THE BEAST
OF KUKUYO

KEVIN JARED HOSEIN

Blouse & Skirt Books

First published by Blouse & Skirt Books, 2018

Blouse & Skirt Books is an imprint of Blue Banyan Books Ltd.

A CIP catalogue record of this book is available from the National Library of Jamaica

ISBN 978-976-8267-15-3

Cover Design by Ion Communications
Maps and illustrations by Portia Subran

Blue Banyan Books
PO Box 5464
Liguanea PO
Kingston 6
Jamaica, W.I.

www.bluebanyanbooks.com

Thanks are due to CODE, The Burt Award for Caribbean Literature and the Bocas Literary Festival

ACKNOWLEDGEMENTS

For the ones who have seen their beast and realized that it can bleed.

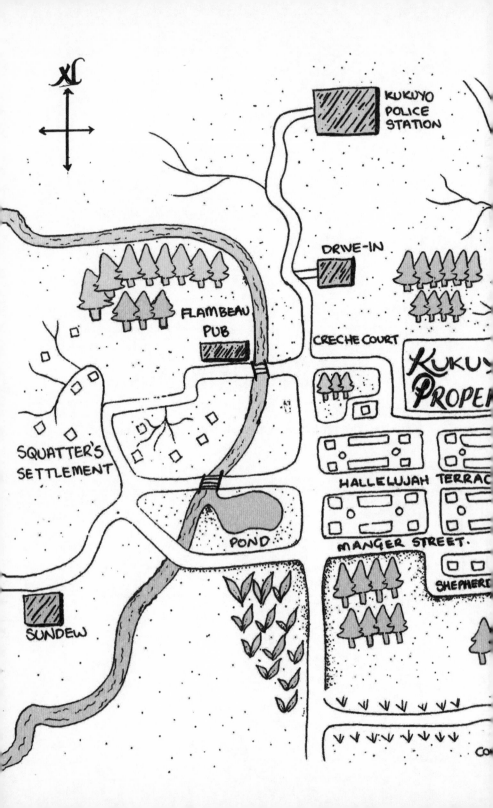

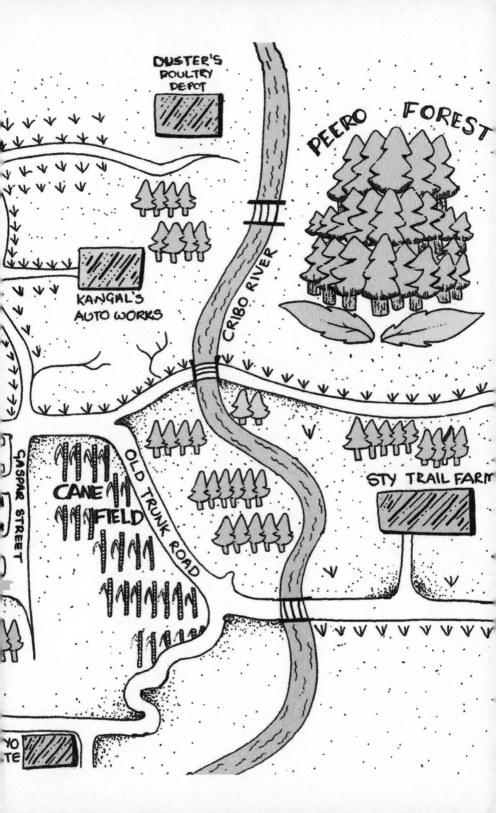

Jessica Fletcher: "You may end up being a character."
David Tolliver: "And what would I be? A victim, a suspect, a killer?"
Jessica Fletcher: "I don't know. I haven't made up my mind yet."

Murder, She Wrote
(Season 1, Episode 5: 'Lovers and Other Killers')

1992, Kukuyo Village, Trinidad.

MOUTH OF THE BEAST

CHAPTER 1

IT COULD MAKE
YOU FEEL LIKE
A STAIN

It come from the dark and take her. That's what they was saying. Dumpling Heera went missing during the power outage. The family didn't realize till the morning come. The bed was empty and the window was closed, glass still intact. They turned the whole house upside-down. She was gone.

Dumpling was her daddy's child and her daddy had money— so on that same day, Kukuyo was under martial law. Everything on lockdown. Everybody had to mind their manners. Uniforms swarming the streets. Flashlights peeping through the slats of every shed, the brambles of every bush. Children packed up their galvanize-sheet wickets and cleared the roads. Nobody got to play after sundown.

I remember watching all of it and thinking, *Nobody going to do all of this if Rune Mathura gone missing.* We was both fifteen-year-old girls, both in the same class, both from the same village. But she was rich and lightskin and live in a big house up in Creche Court. I know it was a bad thing to think, but I think everybody thinks about things like that sometimes. Might as well be honest here. If it was me or anybody who look like me, it wouldn't be no front-page news.

Things went on like that for four nights.

On the second night, they found a pair of denim shorts in one of the drains at the crossroads of Gaspar Street. The mother barely looked at it, told the police it ain't belong to Dumpling.

On the third night, there was another power outage. The blackouts was getting more and more frequent. There was some groundwire problem, the people said—they always take a million years to fix things like that in Kukuyo. The village was different in the moonlight. Dark blue. You could see the stars and the dust swirling from the roads like phantoms over the bushes. In the darkness, the coconut trees in the distance stretched like serpents. You coulda hear strange things in the darkness—things that wasn't there. Groans from the slagheaps, pounding from the water tanks, pitter-pattering from beneath the road.

The night she disappear, I was supposed to be there at her house. Me and Dumpling never talk much before she had the misfortune of getting lumped in with me to do a project on the Spanish and Incans. We just had to do a part on the battle between Atahualpa the Inca ruler and Pizarro the conquistador, whose name always made me hungry for pizza. The project wasn't due for three weeks but Dumpling was the kinda person to get things done early. But she called at the last minute, telling me not to bother come. She ain't say why. I ain't going to lie—I wasn't bad at school but Dumpling was on a whole different level. I thought I was just holding things back.

Mr. and Mrs. Heera never make me feel welcome either. They never said it out loud but I know they didn't want me in the house. Me and Dumpling had to do our work on the porch. I suppose they thought I woulda be dragging grime across their carpet. Maybe I woulda lift my leg up and pee on the furniture. Even my best friend, Tiki—his father ain't never like me. Constantly warned Tiki about *darkskin coolie gals* like me. *See that Rune Mathura?* he used to say. *Gals like she does make man end up in hospital!*

You could be fair, fairer than fair, whiter than the clouds, paler than a corpse and you could get the royal treatment. But if you was dark, you might as well be dirt to some people. You might as well be a shadow. I knew not everybody think this way. But the few who do, it could mess you up. It could make you feel like a stain. Like you know you was out of place standing next to somebody lightskin. You ain't need someone to hold up a mirror to you or show you a photo of it—you just know deep down you was spoiling the scenery.

So it wouldn't have been no surprise to me if the Heeras felt the same way.

Dumpling was always nice to me, though. She was one of them girls you would hate almost immediately when you see them. The girl was pretty, smart and rich. What it had not to hate? Even the shadows under her neck had a glow. She had a little falling out with Mrs. Heera while we was doing our work. Her mother had come out and called her inside. I shifted a little so I could hear.

"Go change your clothes right now, young lady," the mother said.

Dumpling was wearing a coral-pink crop top with denim cutoffs. I wasn't wearing much more than that—a white vest with some old cargo pants rolled up above my knees. I mean, this is Trinidad. We wasn't going to see the Queen of England or nothing.

Dumpling just shook her head. "Mom, we're in the tropics—"

"It looks dreadful."

"Mom, nobody is here. Nobody is watching—"

Then I hear—*whap!* And Dumpling shriek out. I jumped, gritting my teeth. I didn't want to turn around, pretended I didn't hear nothing. My gaze was on old smelly Salaman, who was there to paint the front gate. The slap had catch his attention too. The mother then hiss out, "Cover up your puppies! God is watching!"

Dumpling went in and changed. When she came back, I saw the handprint on her cheek, but she went on like nothing had happen. I didn't expect nothing else. I suppose she was afraid I would tell people. It must be tiring to keep up appearances. Always a snake in every Garden of Eden, I guess.

She was even nice to Salaman, who was still looking our way. He went back to painting once she took her seat. Salaman live over in this big brokedown house on Gaspar Street. People used to call it the madhouse. He had no family. People mostly left Salaman alone. Never ask him for nothing, never invited him to nothing, never offered him prasad for Divali. He had the appearance of a hobo, with long, tousled grey hair that looked like it coulda been washed with muddy river water. His beard was matted, peppered with dank yellow, long enough to shade the muck on his neck. He knew who had money because he used to sweep up the front of every rich family's house. Some of the storefronts as well. If he was lucky, he woulda get to mow a lawn or slap some paint around like he was doing now.

He had an MGA Roadster, which they say he inherited. People was always telling him that he coulda sell it for a small fortune and wouldn't have to be sweeping and scrunting. He barely drove it anyway. He always smiled and shook his head at people who suggested it though. There was plenty stories about him but they was so strange that it was hard to believe them. I mean, we didn't know the man's real name or nothing—I don't think anybody did.

Dumpling brought the man cream soda and a radio to listen to while he worked. It make me think about myself a little. I wasn't nice to much people back then. Looking back, I feel like people hardly ever gave me a chance to be nice.

She fixed her gaze on an illustration of the Incans, how they was all dressed in feathers and fancy patterns as they was dancing and carrying their leader up the road to Cajamarca. "You know what this remind me of?" she said, biting her fingernail. "When you all were little, every Carnival Monday morning, you and the other children used to put on these monster masks and go around house to house. But you used to skip ours."

She was talking about *jab-jab*, where we used to dress up in old clothes and pound broomsticks against the road. We went house to house doing this and the people would pay us to go away. Not much. Maybe ten cents. Twenty-five if you was lucky and early. That was the thing. We stayed out of Creche Court and the squatter settlement. "Want me to be honest?" I tell her. "Didn't make sense expecting money from people who was too rich or too poor."

"I understand." She bowed her head, giving a tiny, embarrassed smile. "I used to wish I could join in."

I shook my head. "The whole thing was kinda stupid. At the end of the day you only had like five dollars in your pocket."

"The money don't matter." As she said that, it come to mind that only a rich girl would say something like that. I know it was bad to think that. Then she asked, "Which one were you?"

"What you mean?"

"Which mask?"

"I was a pirate woman," I replied.

"Alma Reese used to be with you all, right?"

"Just once."

"And your boyfriend was the werewolf, right?"

I began to laugh—more out of nervousness than anything. "Boyfriend? You mean Tiki?" I was shocked that she woulda even notice something like that. Before this project, she never even say a word to me, but I try to keep it straight. "It ain't like that," I tell her. "It ain't have no name for what we have."

"What does that mean?"

"We just have the habit of spending time together. We could get by the night talking shit, playing rummy and speed, trying to record the latest songs on old cassettes. Some nights we carry the radio down to the drive-in and sit on the hill and take in a movie. Tiki knows the FM code to get the audio. When the batteries run out, we have to guess what the people are saying. Last week we catch *Beauty and the Beast*."

I was spilling out more details than I shoulda, but I didn't feel like I shouldn't be. Something felt right about talking to her. I can't say me and Dumpling was friends. But I know right then I wanted to be. I felt like being round her woulda be good for me. Make me a better person.

"You two sound like a couple," she said, letting a smile break through.

I shrugged. "I suppose I can't stop you from thinking that."

Dumpling started playing with her toes. Then she said, "You know, I never had anything like that. I feel like there's nothing for me here."

"Nothing?"

She pull her knees up to her belly, then looked me right in the eye. "I feel like if I run away, I could start over."

My first instinct was to laugh but I held back. I knew where she was coming from. But it make me nervous that she was trying to connect. She had to be desperate, how unashamed she was to be making this confession. Maybe I just catch her at some rare, vulnerable time. I dunno. All I know is that I felt strangely flattered. It's hard to talk to people, to be real with them. You never know who they gonna tell. Still, I had no words for her. I just sat there, fixing my gaze on her. Finally I said, "Running don't solve anything."

I could tell she was disappointed by my response. Perhaps she thought I woulda understand. I mean, she was right. I did. At least I think I did. She had money, she was pretty, she could probably be with anybody or be anything she want to be in the future. Nobody bully her in school—didn't have to deal with no nicknames like Rat. Then some people would just laugh and ask what the hell a fifteen-year-old rich girl have to run from, that life is still good and you should wait till you have a mortgage and bills to pay. Truth is, you could be all of that and still feel alone and empty and fed up. You can't tell anyone because they would just make you feel guilty.

But I wasn't brave enough to say anything else. Couldn't find the right words, though I feel now that the words didn't have to be right. I just stayed quiet, my bottom firm against my seat—like I was waiting for airplane turbulence to stop. I just remember for the rest of that day I had it on my mind how much impact you can have when someone put themselves in front of you like that—especially when you ain't even realize.

My brother, Nick, came home with the story on the fourth night. He was stale-drunk and stammering all over the place so I didn't know if to take him serious at first. He hear the story from Raja, who hear it from somebody working in the car yard, who hear it from somebody up at the police station.

So I'm just telling you like how he tell me.

Up on a hill not too far from Kukuyo was a poultry farm. It was run by old man Duster and his son, Lambi. It was just them and a Doberman named Mangeshkar. People called the dog Mangeshkar the Castrator because she was train to bite people's balls. Had a bandit from Penal who make the mistake of trespassing once—I don't think he coulda have children after what Mangeshkar do to him. Duster was in the papers for that. The journalist quote him as saying, *It feel good to do some good in this world.*

Duster had a daughter a long time ago but she get the salmonella and he claim *black people* up at the hospital kill the girl. My grampa Sam went to the wake. He say the mother went mad and started shoving dirt in her mouth. She died not too long after. Children used to say Duster kill her but that was bogus, I think. Sam said she gave herself a heart attack.

But Sam never deny that they used to treat the chickens better than that woman.

Lambi ain't never finish primary school—say the teacher used to beat him too much because he coulda barely read. But I remember the story going round was that they kick him out because he used to sneak into the girls' toilet to watch them pee. He been working on the farm ever since.

Nick didn't say if the boy was hunting or anything, just that he was out. This was in the early morning, in a glade right past the bridge at Cribo River at the foot of the colossal, unruly Peero Forest. The river was only a five-minute walk from the car yard.

"So Mangeshkar chasing after this agouti and Lambi chasing Mangeshkar," Nick said. "And the agouti dig he way into this hole, scattering the leaves outta the way. This was when Lambi see what he see ..."

My heart was busting out of my chest by then and a part of me wanted to cuff Nick right in the face for how he was prattling off the details. Like it was entertainment. Like it was barstool talk. And I was sure when Raja tell it to him, he did it this exact way like he had the story of the century or something. From how excited he was, I knew the end already.

When Lambi got closer, he coulda see the outline of a foot. A tiny foot sticking up from the ground.

Then the ring of beetles lining it like a thin black anklet.

Take him a while to accept that the foot was human.

He wanted to bolt straight home, but he couldn't. He say it was like a jumbie take hold of him—like he step outside his own body. The dog rush over to the foot, wedging its snout between the toes. Its hind legs scraping against the grass in a tug-o-war as it bite down on the ankle, dragging, dragging.

Lambi didn't have the stomach to pull the girl out.

When the police arrive, they had to bring a backhoe.

It was so twisted, Nick say, it was like it get wedge into the hole with a giant screwdriver.

Big men cry when they see the body.

Dumpling had been found.

CHAPTER 2

SHE IN A BETTER PLACE NOW, AT LEAST

Hallelujah Terrace, where Tiki lived, mighta been only two streets away but actually getting into his room was a whole other story. It required some acrobatics. Behind the house was a bushy, lizard-trodden plot of land. I had to make my way there, scale the backyard fence, climb up the tool shed and pull myself up through Tiki's window from there. Tiki say I'm just like a cat. I kinda liked it, climbing through the window. Even if I coulda waltz in through the front door, I'd pick the acrobatics.

Mister Kangal, as Tiki's father demand you call him, was a real asshole. Tiki took nothing after him so it was strange to think they was even related. Girls liked Tiki but I don't think they coulda hold his interest. I was the only one he really talk to. Same with me—he was one of the only people I spoke to at school. He came out fair like his mother. He had bushy hair, thick sideburns and a goatee. He had it like that because beneath it all, he had the face of a cherub. And he hated that.

Mr. Kangal now, he had a face like stone, almost frozen in that squint-eyed expression you see old men make when they get done downing a shot of whisky. When the rum was in the old man's blood, he slept like a baby. But if he was to wake from that stupor, God forbid, you'd know it by the growl. The growling come deep from his guts. *Mowww*—like a cow in pain. Or a volcano before eruption.

I always heard it before Tiki. And I'd pelt myself under the bed faster than a buttered bullet.

"The hell you makin all that noise in the middle of the night?" the man would say, smacking Tiki on the back of his head. "You wah gimme heart attack? You wah me dead a early death, boy?"

That would be a good day, I'd think to myself.

On the bad days, Tiki wore jeans to cover up the welts. The mother never used to say anything about it. She'd just turn up the volume on the TV. *Matlock* in one room, leather belt dancing in the other. Tiki coulda never be serious with me about what was going on. He would always tell me not to worry about it. I once offer to put a scorpion in his father's shoes—but that kinda talk just get Tiki upset. That was the kinda person he was.

When I got up to the window, he reached down, pulling me in. Before he could say anything, it come out of my mouth, "Dumpling. You hear?" I asked because Raja was Tiki's cousin. I figured both Raja and Nick was running helter-skelter with this news but judging from Tiki's confused expression, it seem like it was me who was running helter-skelter with it. So I tell him, "She's dead. Someone kill her." He didn't say anything. He didn't ask how it happen, how I knew, nothing like that. He just sat on the bed. I sat on the floor.

He brushed his hair from his eyes. Then he said, "I thought she just run away with the boyfriend."

"What boyfriend? She didn't have no boyfriend."

"You sure? Some red man who already outta school. Everybody thought she just run away with him."

"Where the hell you hear this?"

"I dunno. In school—"

"Because that sound like some crap Alma Reese woulda make up." Just a month back, it feel like Alma was telling everybody in Kukuyo Composite that I went around with a maxi conductor, of all things. I was mad like hell when I find out and Tiki had to calm me down, tell me it was just words. But these things—it have a point where it's not just words. Even when they turn out to be lies, people still have the images in their head. "Since when you listening to that liar?" I asked him.

"You know, my gramma had something to say bout liars."

He was just shitting around now. But still, I humour him. I asked, "What's that?"

"Liars could tell the truth. They just dunno they telling it."

I ruffled his hair. "I'll keep that in mind the next time Alma call you a fag."

He reach over and play-punch me. "You better watch your mouth, eh!" He then purse his lips. I could see the way he swallow hard before he asked, "How she die?"

I tell him what Nick tell me—about Lambi, about Mangeshkar, about the foot sticking up from the ground. And it was only while I was saying it out loud that I feel the gravity of it. Dumpling wasn't just dead. She was robbed of life, probably being cut up with knives and scalpels as I sat there and spoke. Someone out there would try to find something uplifting to say, some angle. That she's at rest now; that she's in a better place. But there was nothing uplifting about going to God this way.

"You think the police still there?" I asked.

"Probably there for the rest of the night," he said, giving me a look as if he knew what I was going to say next.

"I gonna go check out the scene," I said, putting my hair in a ponytail. He threw his hands up. I was already at the window. "You coming?"

"This ain't *Murder, She Wrote*, you know."

Murder, She Wrote was a big show back then. Jessica Fletcher was my hero. I think Dumpling deserve someone like that. In Trinidad, the dead are cursed. Nobody remember you after a week. Even if they mangle your body and stuff it in a hole, everybody would just nod their head and say, *We hafta trust in God's plan*. I was done with that. I seen it already. I went through it myself.

Tiki met me outside with his bike. I had my own but this time we rode on the one bike—I was light enough for him to tow me at the front. The bridge over the river was block off by police tape. It was so dark you coulda barely see beyond the bridge. I wasn't expecting to discover nothing different. I felt like I needed to see it for myself. I guess part of me still wasn't believing it.

I nudge Tiki to tell him that we could go now. But he was still, stone-quiet, staring into the gaping mouth of darkness before us, the sounds of the forest slowly spilling out.

"I used to be here with Raja and my other cousins when they used to catch crayfish here," he muttered. "Nick used to be here too. When they stop catching crayfish and start catching girls instead, they ban me from coming."

"What?"

"You know, they used to bring girls," he said, brushing his hair behind his ears. "Right under this bridge." I just nodded, trying not to picture it, then slapped a mosquito off my neck. Tiki then add, "Lambi used to watch. He woulda just show up. Got his ass beat real good one day. That's how he get them front teeth knock out."

My eyebrows shoot straight up. "You serious?"

"They used to call themselves the Billy Goats Gruff. I thought you of all people woulda know."

"Why you thought that?"

"Because Nick was there when it happen. And it was Sam who had to take the boy to the health centre," he said, clicking his tongue. "I dunno much else. Raja ain't like to talk about it. You sure your brother never mention it?"

I shook my head. If Raja ain't like to talk about it, Nick wouldn't bring it up. Nick woulda swing a cricket bat at a lagahoo for that boy.

Tiki returned the shrug. "Maybe Lambi kill Dumpling for all you know."

"You really think so?" I asked, biting my fingernails.

Tiki scrunch up his brow. "I was joking." He pulled his arm away. But I wasn't sure if it was a joke. Tiki then try to change the topic, "They never bring any girls back here once they find out what Lambi was doing though." He paced in a circle around the path, then stopped at the riverbank. He stared into the darkness as if expecting something to emerge. Then he said, "Poor Dumpling. She in a better place now, at least."

I was a little taken aback by this. And his tone—like what's done is done. Same shit, different day. I told you, I been through this before. My father died before I coulda even remember. I only knew my mother. They wasn't even married. When I was about eight, she was stab in the face, her body flung in the bushes. They cremate her without ever finding out who was the culprit. Like the world just wanted to move on and wanted me and Nick to move on with it, as quick as possible. Like she ain't never exist. Never had no reason why. It happen just like that. I felt like there was no moment of silence. So yes, I been through this before.

Nick took the death harder than me. Nick was my mother's son. He had her almond-sliver eyes and her straight nose. He was her shadow. He couldn't sleep. And when he did sleep, he'd wake up in a frenzy, say it was like he was drowning—like his heart about to blow up. The doctor couldn't do nothing. Boss Das, our neighbour, spoke to Sam and told him he knew an old pundit living in a settlement a few miles away. He say the pundit could give Nick a *jharay*—imagine the diet version of *The Exorcist*. The pundit woulda put Nick in a room and circle him with a satchel of bird peppers and garlic cloves and scrape his back with a bundle of broomsticks to drive the jumbie out. Sam didn't end up sending Nick. And not long after that, he stop having the nightmares. At least, so he say.

I suppose there mighta been a time you could get Nick to talk about our mother. But that was long gone. *She in a better place.* That was something Nick woulda say. He'd snap and say it, as if he was really just meaning to tell you to shut up.

I said to Tiki, "When somebody screw you down into a hole, I'll tell them you in a better place."

He raised his eyebrows but didn't say anything, just nodded. I think he realized I was upset and just didn't want to say anything else. Sometimes it's hard to say the right thing so you just say anything. I understand. I just stood there, still looking into the darkness, with that same thought I have whenever a memory of my mother cross my mind—that they was still out there, whoever do it. The weight of that stayed on my heart all the way back to bed.

CHAPTER 3

SOMETHING OFF WITH EVERYBODY IF YOU REALLY THINK BOUT IT.

The news people rush down to Kukuyo early the next morning. They pulled up in white vans leaving trails of dust behind. All the children flock to them like they was giving away ice cream. Most of them kept their distance, aiming their cameras at the cane fields between Gaspar Street and Old Trunk Road, the muddy roads and the knee-high lawns on Hallelujah Terrace and around my own house on Shepherd Street. They was snapping photos of signs on vendor stalls and walls all along Manger Street: *Tomatoe Juice. Breakfass Shed. Pig Tale for Sale.*

They interviewed a few of the villagers. I think Sam was upset they didn't talk to him. He even had his hat on for the whole day and wore his favourite plaid, red lumberjack shirt. Samardeep Mathura was just a day over seventy but never liked to be called grampa or nana or nothing like that. Sam was what he want you to call him, no matter who you was. You coulda be Saddam Hussein or the Sai Baba of Shirdi, Sam was what he wanted you to call him.

That evening, Boss Das park himself on the hassock while Sam was on his recliner. I sat on the floor, my hip against his ankle. Nick was cross-legged on the floor, closest to the TV. Never mind that Das was our neighbour, I used to be afraid of him when I was smaller—the man looked like he coulda wrestle a bison. He was bald with the remaining hair forming the shape of a horseshoe but still had this tuft of grey above his forehead, almost looking like a rhino horn. His wife never really spoke to us. She had a mean old face, always had this look like she just suck a lime. Das used to just describe her as a difficult woman. I suppose that's why he was always coming over whenever he had the chance.

"You all ain't popping no popcorn?" Nick said. I coulda tell he had a couple drinks in him from Flambeau but he wasn't full on drunk. There was a time when he did his drinking in secret. He'd started raiding Sam's cane rum collection a few years back—that's the first I know of it. Sam never used to drink them so he wasn't missing them when they was gone. We didn't know till the school catch Nick with a half bottle of Old Cask in his bag, lying right next to his textbooks. That same afternoon, Sam threw all of it in the garbage, every last bottle of the collection. But that didn't stop Nick from getting alcohol. He just knew not to bring it under Sam's roof.

"Somebody better be taping by the time I come on," Nick said.

"What you mean?" I asked him. "The people talk to you?" I didn't see anybody interview Nick.

Sam leaned forward. "They talk to you, of all people?"

"Nick taking care of business, man," Das said, giving a small smile.

Nick let out a chuckle. "I make sure and put on perfume and everything."

Sam laughed. "What you put on perfume fer? They could smell you through the TV?"

"I hope you rinse out your mouth too," Das said.

Sam suck his teeth, falling back into his recliner. I wasn't sure if Nick was joking. I didn't say anything though. Hopefully whatever footage of the madman rant he probably make, they forget on the cutting room floor. Not that Nick wasn't a reliable storyteller—just that he probably wasn't the best person to tell it.

"Nick, what you say to the people?" I asked him.

"Rune, you shoulda talk to them," Sam said. "You and the girl was friends."

Nick spin to me. "I ain't know you was friends—"

"We was working on—"

Nick slap his forehead. "Shit, girl—you coulda tell me that! I woulda tell them!"

"We wasn't really—"

"Shush!" Nick said, turning back to the TV. "Look it starting!"

A wide shot of Kukuyo panned across the TV before focusing on the field reporter. She had brown highlights and had on a pinstripe pantsuit. She was one of the more popular ones. It was a sight. You didn't see women dressed like that here. "That is the one you talk to, Nick?" I asked.

Nick nodded. "She almost give me her number. True talk."

"She will rock you and burp you when you pass out on the floor, I'm sure," I said.

But Nick wasn't listening.

Dumpling came up on the screen, a photo of her in a white sari. Nick leaned closer to the screen. It was weird seeing her on the TV. It looked like an old photo, like when she was back in Form One. It almost threw me off when they called her Devi, her real name. Devi Heera.

Das raised his eyebrows. "Sammy, boy, look at how nice and lightskin that girl was. That is Kashmir blood right there."

Nick said, "Well, if she was like we, it wouldn't have all this news crew swoopin down like seagulls." Sam shook his head, unamused. I agreed with Nick, as distasteful as the comment was.

"You all ain't find she looking like that actress?" Nick asked. "The one in the Amitabh Bachchan movie. It was in the cinema a few months back." He kept snapping his fingers, trying to remember.

Sam squinted at him. "What you talkin about, boy?"

"Is Sridevi Kapoor you talkin bout, Nick?" Das said.

Nick pointed at Das, beaming wide. "Yeah, yeah! That's the one!" The lights suddenly started to flicker. It was that flicker you look out for when the power was about to go. "Jeezus!" Nick let out, getting up from the floor, fists up as if bracing himself for a blow. "If this blasted current decide to go now ..."

But then the lights went back to normal and Nick took his seat.

The camera cut back to the reporter, who was now standing in the middle of the street, the Heera house in the background. It then showed big-bottom Fatima next to her. Fatima was wailing, spitting against the microphone. I was cringing with each word. "I say we need a curfew! This Minister of Security we have doin a bunch of *jhanjhat!* If this did happen to *anybody* child in this present Gov-ah-ment, you woulda see action already. But here? We catchin we tail to even get proper electricity in this place."

Sam said, rubbing his forehead, "I can't believe they give this woman airtime."

"Sammy, that is Salaman I seein there?" Das cut in, pointing at the TV.

It really was him. He was in the background, sweeping up a storm on the sidewalk with a cocoyea broom while Fatima continued her tirade. Sam had nothing to say except, "The whole country probably laughing right now. They ain't studying that a lil girl get kill."

"Probably he kill the girl," Nick throw in. "Just like how he cut off that man head."

It was a primary school legend. I never heard the story being toss around elsewhere. Nobody coulda say how true it was. There wasn't no details or backstory. Just that Salaman clean cut off a man's head with a cutlass like it was the top of a coconut. Funny enough, I never bothered to ask Sam about it. Sam looked down on gossip like that.

"That is a bogus story," Sam said, shaking his head.

"You never know, eh, Sam," Das replied, clicking his tongue. He then turned to me. "We was lil boys when that happen."

Sam sat up. "Yeah but nobody know what really went down."

"Who head he cut off?" I asked.

"The sardar," Sam answer. "Allegedly."

"Sardar?"

"The man with the whip." Sam pretend to be cracking one.

Das told the story. "The sardar take in Salaman when he was a lil boy and leave him the house when he dead. Well, how the sardar dead—they find he head floatin in the river. They never find the body. That Roadster that Salaman have. Classic car. That basically become his after the man dead."

Nick cut in, "He probably kill him for it."

"Salaman really kill him?" I asked. It was easier to throw these questions at Das.

Das replied, "Well, if you was around back then, you woulda know why the sardar take in a young boy like Salaman. Had all manner of stories bout that man, how he use to put Salaman in a rainwater barrel whenever he act up. Leave him in there for two days without no food or nothin. Remember that, Sammy?"

Sam slouched, his mouth in a disgusted grimace.

"Well, nobody ain't like to talk bout it," Das added, giving a shrug. "Nobody ain't like to say they know what was happenin in that house and ain't do nothin bout it."

"Just be wary out there. End of story," Sam uttered out, turning to me. "You better watch yourself, how you does be going all over the place with that Kangal boy." Sam fully well knew Tiki's name but always insisted on calling him the Kangal boy to irritate me.

It wasn't that Sam didn't like Tiki. I think he was afraid Tiki would do to me what Raja do to Nick. The Kangals were notorious drunks and troublemakers. Low-class, garbage behaviour, Sam called it. Their legacy was to camp out in front of Flambeau at five o' clock in the morning waiting to guzzle rum till noon. The only one who had a lick of sanity was Tiki's uncle, who owned the car yard. He probably employed half the Kangal clan since they couldn't get no other work. Raja never got drunk when Nick was around. I think it was some kind of weird show of power—that he had control and Nick didn't. That he was better than Nick. Nick drank enough for the two of them anyway. The yard doubled up as a rehab centre because you had to promise to sober up if you wanted to keep your job there. They did repairs, power washing, the works. As much as it pain Sam, he always encouraged Nick to try to get a steady job there. For him to try and do something with himself. But other than that, Sam didn't want us to have nothing to do with any of them.

"So when the wedding is?" Das asked me, breaking out in a grin.

Sam leaned towards Das. "Don't be giving the girl no ideas. I have an obligation to these two children. I have to make sure at least one of them turn out proper."

"We ain't lil children again, old man Sam," Nick said, a serious look on his face. "We big enough to wipe we own ass and have we own friends."

Nick was brave to talk to Sam that way. He was probably the only person in Kukuyo who could've. I suppose Sam was used to it by now. "I'll alert the media," was all Sam replied, sucking his teeth.

Das asked, "How old you is, Nick?"

"Sweet seventeen."

"Seventeen is the age to be, man," Das say. "Live it up! I wish I was seventeen again."

I believed Sam had given up on trying to change Nick. Sam couldn't tell Nick nothing because Nick didn't even believe he had a problem. Addiction is a funny thing. People think of it as the body craving something and it want this thing so bad that it begins to throw tantrums just like how a spoil child might throw himself on the ground and flail around till his limbs hurt. But I think it's more of an emotional thing. If a person isn't at peace with their thoughts, anything could take over. One thing lead to another. I feel like Nick was addicted to the bottle before he even take his first sip.

Lambi came on the TV screen. Nick flung himself backwards on the floor, exclaiming, "Like they pulling names outta a barrel!"

"Well, Nick, he discover the body, you know," I tell him.

Das patted his shoulder. "They probably saving the best for

last."

As the interview went on, Das squinted his eyes at the TV and said, "Something was always off bout this boy. This is Duster son, right?"

Sam shrugged. "Something off with everybody if you really think bout it. I mean, the boy ain't too right in the head. The mother wasn't neither. Duster trying his best."

Das scratched his chin. "So this is the fella who find the body? How them know he ain't kill the girl heself?"

At that same moment, Lambi looked right into the camera and gave a smile. Two front teeth missing. Then I recalled how they got knock out.

"It wouldn't surprise me," Nick said. "The fella is a serious perv."

I kept Tiki's story in mind. I wanted to ask him what he mean by that, as if I was completely oblivious to the story. But I didn't want to do it with Sam around.

They was filming the house again. Salaman was still sweeping in the background. The reporter's voiceover concluding the story. It seem that was it. Nick didn't get on the TV after all. He was stone-silent. That's when you know he was upset—when he would just sit there like nothing affect him. He got up, saying he was going to the toilet, but I knew exactly where he was going. If he had to go to the toilet, he woulda just went. Anytime he announced it, it was because he wanted to go to Sam's old workshed at the back of the house.

Sam did repairs. Lawn mowers, stereos, TV's, things like that. That's why he was so respected in the village. Because we all make mistakes and things always get broken. We neglect things and let them rust. It's good knowing there's somebody who can make things whole again. Well, it was Sam himself who come up with that line. He thought all jobs had a kinda nobility and sacredness to it. Farmers had to appreciate how things grow and thrive. Bakers, with their ovens perpetually full and empty, had to know their bread was always bringing comfort and sustenance. I suppose this was why Sam was always pushing Nick to get a job at the car yard, despite it being infested with the Kangal clan. Perhaps he thought that sense of purpose and being could stave off the alcohol.

When Sam wasn't using the shed, Nick occupied it, taking apart old stereos and Walkmans and microwaves. I dunno why he did it. I suppose he found a kinda peace in it—disassembling and laying out the parts on the bench. Screws and transistors and copper contacts. That wasn't what he was going to do now though. He had a bottle of Jose Cuervo Blanco tequila hidden under a loose floorboard. This is what it had come to. In the middle of the night, Nick shut himself in the shed and drank. I only knew because he forgot to put it back under the board one night. I did it for him because I didn't want to see Sam and Nick fight.

I followed him into the shed and came in just as he was pulling the bottle out of the floorboard. Honestly, I expected him to stop once he saw me come in. But all he said was, "Sam see you come in?"

"He watching the news still."

"Well, you ain't seeing nothing here."

I let out a sigh. "I wish I wasn't seeing nothing here."

He pouted, sounding annoyed all of a sudden, "What the hell you want?" He set the bottle down on the workbench.

I folded my arms. "How come you call Lambi a perv?"

He paused. "Everybody know the fella is a perv."

"Yeah but I want to know about the incident near Cribo River. At the bridge."

He took a long slow sip of the tequila. "Look. That was a long time ago."

"Why you don't want to tell me?"

He narrow his eyes at me, then took another sip. "The bridge was a popular spot to carry girls. That perv used to come outta nowhere and frighten them away. We know he wasn't too right in the head. Probably never had a girl for heself. We just thought it woulda be funny if we put together some money to have Gonorrhoea Gayatri feel him up—do stuff with him—to see how he woulda react. Raja had arrange the whole thing."

I hesitate a little but still asked, "And what happen?"

"I dunno. She kick him in the face or something. Break his nose, knock two of his front teeth straight out. You have to ask Raja. I wasn't really watchin when it happen. We didn't know what to do cause he was bloody up pretty bad. We happen to see Sam and—"

"Where you get that bottle, boy?" a voice said from behind us. It was Sam, standing tall, arms folded. He reached his arm out, waiting for Nick to hand him the tequila.

Nick couldn't look the man in the eye. He glared at me instead. "Why you had to come in here and mess up the program?" he muttered. He didn't say it mad or nothing. He just sounded tired. He move to take another sip right before Sam snatch the bottle and poured the remains onto the ground.

Sam's voice got gruff. "You could go and do whatever when you outside that gate. Go dip your damn self in breadcrumbs and roll round in dog shit, I ain't care. But if you want to stay under my roof, you better wipe yourself off before you come in."

Nick just sat there, arms on the bench, facing the wall, face puffed up like a frog. "Nick," I said to him. But he wasn't paying me no mind. I dunno what was worse for him—that the tequila was gone or that he'd been caught.

Sam grabbed my hand. I nudged Nick's shoulder and he flung up in a fury and marched right into the road. Sam went after him but realized it was no use. I was two steps behind him. "One day," Sam muttered to himself. "One day it will have no direction to go but up." Perhaps he hadn't really give up on Nick after all.

He looked right in my eyes. "I seeing this my whole life. I lose my father to it. He lose his father to it. Not just the rum. This depression, this mindset. It's like a beast that sink it claws into you. Promise me I ain't going to lose you to it."

"That ain't gonna happen," I said, shaking my head.

He put his head down. "When they bring that boy, Lambi— he was dazed like a truck knock him flat on the road. What them boys do, Nick and them Kangal hooligans, I will never understand it. They couldn't even do him the common courtesy of wiping his face." With those words, he shuffled back inside, hands in his pockets.

CHAPTER 4

IT HAVE AN EPISODE OF MURDER, SHE WROTE ABOUT THAT?

The cremation was at the Shore of Peace. They bus the whole class there. The Principal, Mr. Moonesar, was there too. Moonesar knew it would have plenty cameras there and had to make sure we was all in good manners. Kukuyo Composite was a quiet school and the country should know that—I could imagine him thinking something like that. There was people and police like crazy. The crowd was pouring into the street. The line of cars was never ending. Some men sat in their trunks, dressed like they just stumble out of a chutney fete, pouring puncheon rum into party cups. Others was standing against the walls, blowing cigarette smoke into the breeze. Every Tom, Dick and Harry.

The wooden pyre was centre stage, white *jhandi* pennants dancing behind it. The gulf was extra grey that day. The concrete ground of the site was blotted with ashes and sea salt.

Everybody kept saying that the funeral people had Dumpling looking like new again. Swear, these people coulda put Humpty Dumpty together again, I heard one of them say. They had us walk past to take a look and say goodbye. I couldn't look for long. On her forehead was a thick thumb-stroke of sandalwood paste. Poinsettia petals was planted across her chest. Her body anointed in ghee.

The brother had to help the mother finish perform the *aarti*. Like the father, his head was shaved except for a tiny bob of hair notched at the back. Nobody was referring to her as Dumpling. But it was hard to think of her as Devi Heera. *Diamond of the divine*, they said her name meant.

Diamond, which cannot be shattered.

Divine, which cannot be touched.

I think it was just us at school who used to call her Dumpling. The first day, in Form One, one of the teachers, Mr. Bhagan, call her that by mistake. He realize his mistake immediately—the class totally erupt when his hand shot to his mouth like he had utter a cussword in a temple. He apologized, saying that Dumpling was the nickname for his daughter. So everyone started calling her Dumpling to make fun of the teacher. And the name stuck. But I think the name stuck as well because the girl really did look like a Dumpling, if you can imagine it.

Me and Tiki sat together for the procession. He combed his hair for once. I nudged him with my elbow and pointed my chin at the familiar lanky figure standing amongst the crowd gathered in the road. Lambi. Broiler bloodstains and cigarette ashes on his sleeves.

Tiki gave him a passing glance and shrugged. "It ain't so strange."

I tell him, "Is a little strange to show up to a funeral for someone you dunno."

He shrugged again. "Plenty people here don't know Dumpling. The story was all over the TV." Tiki pointed his chin at a man standing by himself. "Look, even badman Joey here." Joey was young, early twenties. The only way you coulda tell his age was the big *Magnum P.I.* mustache. He was so bony he reminded me of a starved stray pothound—big eyes, small-small mouth. Joey was in and out of Kukuyo. He was born here but moved out when his mother died. The house was empty now but Joey used to come back, tidy it up, cut the grass himself. Tiki say that Joey used to bring his car in at the yard almost every month. Almost every time they found blood on the tyres, the backseat, the steering wheel. But they always shut their mouth and hosed it off.

I fixed my gaze on the body as two men slotted it onto the pyre, the feet facing us. The skin pale and moist, like kneaded bread dough. While two bareback men circled the pyre, I said to Tiki, "Had this episode of *Murder, She Wrote* where this man went on vacation. And he drop dead of a heart attack. The wife wanted to make sure he get cremate—"

"Wait, lemme guess—was the wife who actually kill him."

I had to stop myself from reaching out to ruffle his hair. "Of course. And they never woulda know if they didn't stop the cremation."

"Now you look to bring up this talk? Too late now. Speak now or forever hold your peace."

One of the men dipped a torch over the pyre. The small flame breathed life into a bigger one. The body began to crackle. Skin melting off the bones. Soot rising from the mouth. My eyes was stinging in the smoke. I didn't even know I was holding Tiki's hand the whole time till I see Mr. Moonesar's eyes fall upon us.

I remained silent till the whole thing was done. I looked around at everybody. Each solemn face. In a week, they was gonna forget all of this. I knew the expressions. I seen them during my mother's own cremation. I kept her in mind as the smoke carry itself to the sky. The body was still trying to say something, trying to tell us who robbed the life from it. But everybody just wanted to move on. It was the time of forgetting. Same shit, different day.

After the whole thing was done, I stood near the back of the bus. Alma Reese and Krissy Kanhai was talking. They was the rumour mill, to put it lightly. I usually wouldn't eavesdrop—half of it wouldn't even be true anyway—but I overheard a bit that catch my attention. Krissy was telling Alma, "They was saying she had a mark on the chest. Like a bitemark but it was missin some of the top teeth."

"You talkin shit?" Alma replied. "Who say this?"

"My brother know somebody workin up at the morgue. He say they think it was a bitemark."

"How much teeth?"

"What?"

"How much teeth was missing?"

"I dunno. About two?" Krissy said, starting to sound a little frustrated that she didn't know the details. I was getting a little frustrated too.

"You sure?"

"You asking the wrong person, Alma." She sounded annoyed by then. At the same time, Krissy noticed me behind them. As she pointed her chin to me, Alma spin around and called out to me, "What you sniffing round here for?"

From the corner of my eye, I saw the cameramen packing up. I wasn't even thinking about how I just got caught eavesdropping. All I had in my mind was Lambi's grin. The way he stared into the camera with that hair-raising smile, those front teeth missing. Then I pictured the moment they was kicked out. Him under the bridge with Gonorrhoea Gayatri, curled up, confused, his mouth sour with blood. I wondered what he had tried to do with her.

"Rat! I talkin to you!"

That nickname always had an immediate effect on me. I balled up my fists, gritted my teeth. It wasn't the word itself, you know. It was the manner she used to say it. Like I was something to be scorned. It coulda be any word. To have someone call you a name over and over again, you ain't human if it ain't get to you eventually. It was different from Dumpling. Dumpling liked her nickname—she said so.

Tiki come up to me. I wasn't going to start nothing, not with all these people around, but he had a grip on my arm anyway. "Why you have to jump in the scene so?" Krissy said to him. "Let them handle their business."

Tiki shook his head. "Handle business? Here? Listen. Our classmate just get cremated. The ashes still fresh. No need for this."

Alma came right up to him. "What that have to do with me, fag?"

I let out a grumble. "Cool it," Tiki said. I wasn't sure if he was telling me or Alma.

"That is what you tell your father when he beatin you?"

It amazed me how crap like that don't phase Tiki. He could hear shit like that and smile it off. I had to be angry for the both of us. He patted my shoulder and guided me back to the bus.

"You know how Lambi missing two front teeth?" I whisper to him as we took our seats. He looked at me, furrowing his brow, waiting for me to make my point. I continued, "They say that Dumpling had a bitemark on her chest. And that the bitemark was missing two teeth."

Tiki then looked at me as if he was halfway expecting me to laugh and tell him I was joking. "It have an episode of *Murder, She Wrote* about that?" he asked, chuckling.

That was when I shoulda come to my senses. The amount of shit that come outta Alma mouth was staggering. But it wasn't Alma telling Krissy. It was Krissy telling Alma. Dunno if that really make a difference but the signal was clear in my head. Like my Spidey sense was tingling. Still—the shit that used to pass between Alma and Krissy—some of it was true sometimes. But before I coulda say anything, Tiki said, "You know how much people in this place missing teeth, Rune? Even Sam missing teeth."

I put my hand on his shoulder. "You ain't think Lambi guilty, right?"

"No."

"So who you think kill Dumpling?"

"How you expect me to know that?"

"You think the family do it?"

"No," he said. "I dunno."

"You think Alma do it?"

"No. What is your—"

"What about Joey?"

He shuffled in his seat. "I dunno. Don't ask me bout Joey."

"My point is you dunno nothing about Lambi either but you

already write him off, more than everybody else." Tiki was quiet after that. "How you explain that?"

But he just shrugged it off. "Well, we dunno enough. We can't just pass judgment when we dunno enough."

I didn't say nothing after that because I knew Tiki woulda just keep fighting me down. I remained convinced that I was onto something.

Later that night, me, Sam, and Boss Das sat down to watch the news. Nick was missing in action. "How much cameras it had, Rune?" Das asked. "You make sure to look at the camera when they was filmin you?"

But Dumpling's funeral got pushed all the way to the end of the newscast, just before they went to sports. Now, the big story was in the city. Just as I predict, Trinidad sidelined Dumpling and latch on to the next big thing. An old woman's throat was slit three times after two men broke into her house. Police say it was a robbery.

"Robbery, my ass," Das said, sucking his teeth. He leaned over to Sam. "Which bandit would slit somebody throat just like that? Is money they want—they not lookin to slit nobody throat."

Sam shook his head. "Is a different country now, Das."

Das let out a scoff. "Lemme tell you somethin. Remember that holdup it had in the Chinee restaurant near Indian Walk last week? I hear this woman was a witness. She see the bandit and them number plate before they gone in! And she make the mistake of givin the police the info. Well, look at how you could catch a death now for doin the right thing, nuh! They ain't gonna tell you that in the news, though."

"Rune, you hear that?" Sam turned to me. "If you see any funny business, you tell Sam first. Don't be no hero!" This was why I couldn't always listen to Sam. This was the same man who tell me that mosquitoes only lay eggs in stagnant water—that you had to be a river, always flowing, always going somewhere. And now he was saying the right thing was doing nothing. I respected Sam but sometimes he didn't know what the hell he was talking about.

CHAPTER 5

RUNE, YOU'RE A SICK PERSON, YOU KNOW THAT?

Me and Tiki used to ride our bikes to school. We used to meet up under the old water tower at the edge of Kukuyo proper and go from there along Old Trunk Road, where the cane fields was. Then after school we'd go right back there. It was our safe spot, you could say. It wasn't so safe lately though, at least since the bats started making a home there. I split off the path on the way back home the next day however. "Where the hell you goin?" Tiki called out to me.

"I wanna show you something," I tell him. I didn't say nothing else, just sped up. If I told him, he wouldn't have come. I had the route plotted out in my head from since the morning recess period. We rode past the car yard and all the way up to a muddy knoll.

Only when we got close to the chicken farm and the stench was in the air, Tiki realized what was going on. "Shit, Rune," he said, pinching his nostrils. "You still with this nonsense?"

I couldn't concentrate in class. I couldn't get the funeral outta my mind. The fact that Dumpling was just ashes now. I barely even knew the girl and it seem like I had it harder than people she used to talk to everyday. In history class, I came across the notes me and Dumpling had about the Spanish and Incans. Atahualpa and Pizarro at the battle in Cajamarca in Peru. It was the story of how two hundred Spanish soldiers manage to overthrow the Incan army of eighty thousand. Atahualpa had accepted an invitation from the conquistador to attend a feast. Atahualpa was in the mood for celebration, marching with masqueraders and dancing and singing. He leave his soldiers in the mountains and went with only a few of his people, just to be ambush and captured. He fill rooms with gold for the Spanish but they still burn him at the stake at the end of the day.

I think we was a little like Atahualpa—we in Trinidad who know the bad things are coming and do nothing. There's so much good people out there. The bad is just the minority yet it still lead to the downfall of a great people. You could be good and do nothing. That ain't stopping the ambush from happening.

The track was muddy and lined with tyre patterns and chicken feathers. It was so muddy that we couldn't properly manoeuvre our bikes through it. So we had to roll them up. "Rune, you're a sick person, you know that?" Tiki said. "You know we going to get shoot, right? Duster gonna come right out and blow our heads clean off."

"We ain't going inside, you know."

"You dunno Duster—if we ain't get shoot, he gonna sic Mangeshkar on we. I hear that dog could bite a chicken head clean off."

I laughed. "You think the dog coulda dig a hole and put Dumpling in it?"

Tiki threw his hands up, stopping in his tracks. "You feel this is a joke?"

I stopped too. "I just have my doubts about Lambi."

He looked straight at me. "You still obsessing with this Lambi thing? Why Lambi?"

"Told you already. Lambi was the one who discover the body. And he discover it in the same place he used to spy on all them girls. Dumpling had a bitemark missing teeth. Lambi is missing teeth. He ain't too right in the head. He is a pervert. What other kinda person coulda do this?"

"You talking like you already investigate the boy."

"It worth a shot to see if my theory hold water."

Tiki just shook his head. He knew there was nothing he could say, and I know he was just looking out for me—didn't want me to be doing nothing stupid. We continued up the track. Up ahead was the front gate of the farm. There was somebody in the distance. We was too far to be spotted. We crouched behind a bush, looking ahead.

Tiki's hand was heavy on my shoulder. "Think they see us?"

I shook my head. "Nah. They too far up ahead."

Tiki shifted to the side. "I ain't never going to forgive you if that dog bite my balls off, you hear?"

I chuckled. "Boy, you are too much of a coward."

"Easy for you to say. You don't have balls."

"I have more than you."

I got a snicker outta him with that. As he move to play-punch me, the figure in the distance come into view. It was like something out of a horror show. It was Lambi in his dusty white overalls. Over his shoulder was a crocus bag, stretching to his mid-back. Blood smeared and leaking from it. He looked up at the sky and for a moment, I expected him to howl. He looked feral, like a monster hiding in the dark corner of a dream. Mangeshkar was behind him, slurping at his fingers. He remained still for a while, felt like a minute, just staring off into the distance.

He drop the bag and started to take off his overalls—right there in the middle of the yard.

Tiki nudge my shoulder, whispering, "What the hell he doing?"

I ain't answer. I didn't know. He undress till he was down to just his jockey shorts and toss his overalls up on the fence. He was thin as a knife and his whole chest was cover with tattoos. I couldn't tell what was what from that distance but the one stretching across his shoulder blades looked like a giant eye.

"Rune, let's get outta here."

"Wait." I held Tiki's arm. Lambi picked up the bloody bag and disappeared behind the house, the dog behind him all the way. Only when he was gone did me and Tiki hustle back to our bikes and ride the hell outta there.

We rode till we was back on the path to Kukuyo, at a crossroads leading to the car yard. We stopped at an old samaan tree to catch our breaths. "We gonna go back tonight, see what was in that bag," I told Tiki.

He shot a look at me like I was utterly deranged. "You was seeing what I was seeing, right?"

"Yeah."

"And you gonna go back there—by yourself—in the night time?" He wiped some sweat from his forehead.

"You gonna come with—"

He let out a laugh. "You need help, Rune. Leave me outta this bullshit."

"Tell me the truth. You shit yourself back there?"

He laughed again. "You saying your underwear still clean after what we just see? You have more balls than me, for real. Was nice knowin you."

I wasn't surprised. I knew it was asking too much for him to come. But at least one person had to know where I was going. I said to him, "Thanks for coming with me and seeing it for yourself.

He scoff. "As if I had a choice."

We rode off. Just as we was passing the car yard, I heard a car coming up fast behind us. I was about to swing to the side when the bike chain locked up. I turned around. The car wasn't slowing. Time slowed down as I threw myself to the side of the road onto a tuft of grass. I near damn fall into a ditch. I grazed my knee. Tiki had already swung to the other side. The car mashed brakes—but if I hadn't swung, he woulda knock me right down.

The car pulled over at the side of the road, just a truck's length from me. It was a Buick Regal sedan, cream coat, mahogany brown roof. The driver got out. It was Joey Jodha. He looked at my bike before he looked at me. I saw Tiki from the corner of my eye. He just stayed there, frozen, his hands clutching the handlebars tight. Joey was looking at him now. "Kangal," he said to him.

"Yeah," was all Tiki said.

"Tell your girlfriend to be more careful next time."

Tiki paused. "I will."

He then came up to me and reached his hand down to pull me up. Everything felt quiet at that moment. Like he had willed the wind to stop blowing and the birds to stop chirping. It felt wrong to even touch him. I didn't have no choice though. He pulled me up and set my bike to stand. He looked at me again, as if memorizing my features. He then looked at the bike again. Felt like an eternity before he said something, even though all he said was, "That's a nice BMX."

With those words, he went back to his car. After he drove off, Tiki exhaled loudly. As if he was underwater the whole time. "I dunno how they deal with him down at the yard," he said.

"They shouldn't have to deal with that. That's like they're accessories to a crime, right?"

"You have to be in their shoes," Tiki said, scratching his neck. "Can't just judge them like that. It ain't like they want to be washing blood off. And it ain't like they knew they was gonna have to clean out lil chunks of flesh the first time he bring a car in. What they gonna say to the man now? *Mr. Joey, we don't want no more bloody cars in we yard. Bring another one and we callin the police on you.* You want them get the place burn down? You never know how people like Joey would react to that."

"So the police can't do nothing?"

"You know his father was a big-time piece of shit police, right? He was workin with the coke dealers and them. I dunno if Joey even knew the man till his mother get sick and they was going to lose their home. Before that, Joey's mother never wanted him to know the father, but they needed the money. The rest is history." He cleared his throat. "My uncle shoulda know better than to take up Joey business."

He hop on his bike and I got on mine. Usually he'd ride with me to my house and then go back to his. We went our separate ways when we got back to the village.

CHAPTER 6

GET 'IM! GET 'IM! GET 'IM OR YOU GONNA GET DEAD TONIGHT!

The perfect opportunity fell into my lap that same night. That woman that got her throat slit three times—turned out that Sam and Das went to school with her. The last time he even saw the woman was a hundred years ago but I don't think that matter. It wasn't no normal wake. This was a nine-night with dancing and rum and food. Das convinced Sam to go, said they would drive up there in Das' old Bluebird and come back in the morning. Anything to get away from his wife, I suppose.

Nick was in the shed. I was surprised Sam was still letting him use it. I went to see him.

"What the hell you want?" he blurt out as soon as I walked in, a half-smoked Du Maurier cigarette drooping from his lips, cloud of smoke coming out behind him. A screwdriver and a neatly dissembled RC car was on the dry-rotted workbench. The chorus of Rikki Jai's 'Sumintra' was playing faintly from a radio perched atop the metal lathe. I don't think he had drink anything since the night of the tequila incident. He was a grouch when he didn't drink. He hated the world. And I hate to say it but I preferred how he acted when he was drunk. I feel like he was more liable to do something rash when he was going through the withdrawal. It always made me a little nervous to be around him.

I let him know what I wanted. "Lubricant."

"For what?"

"The BMX feeling a little stiff."

At the same time, Sam came up to the shed. "Me and Das getting ready to go," he said.

Nick took the cigarette out of his mouth, "Rune going with you?"

"No. I leaving you two alone here. Stay home and watch some TV. Don't go nowhere while I ain't here."

Nick turned to me, raising his eyebrows. "You staying home to watch TV with me?"

I wanted to punch him so bad. "*Murder, She Wrote* on tonight," I tell him.

Nick nodded, turning to Sam. "What time you comin back?"

"I comin back when I comin back." He pause, then looked right into Nick's eyes. "I know plenty people thinking that girl they find in the bush—that that was some kinda freak occurrence. But you will have a freak occurrence if you don't listen to me, you hear?"

"I hear you," Nick replied.

When Sam was gone, Nick got the lubricant for me. I pulled my BMX to the side of the house and began slicking up the bike chain. Sam bought the bike for me about two Christmases back with his pension. When he rolled it in, there was a Joker card clipped to the wheel so it could sound like a motorcycle.

He had wrote on the card, *For Arundhati. Keep your balance, keep moving! – Sam.*

The card never left that wheel.

Nick was right next to me, mumbling to himself. He looked at me, shaking his head. "The old man need to cool his shit. He always on my case. Telling you, that man ain't like my face."

I laughed as I continued working on the bike chain. "Sam's just looking out for us."

He looked at me, pursing his lips. "He plain-as-day hate me, I tell you."

I paused working on the chain, gazing up at him. "He ain't hate you," I tell him. "He just don't like you drinking so much."

"Everybody does drink, girl." He grimaced, his eyes falling on the bike. "And where the hell you going anyway?"

"Just gonna go for a ride with Tiki." I got up, dusting myself off.

"So I suppose to stay home and babysit nothing then?" He shrugged, raising his eyebrows, biting his lower lip. "Well, well, it's probably best I just go down to Flambeau tonight since I have nothing else to do." He was just being shitty now, trying to make me feel guilty. It worked for a second, before I realized the goofy look on his face and that if I had stay my ass home and watched *Murder, She Wrote*, Nick woulda been pissing at the side of Flambeau anyway. There wasn't nothing I could do to stop that.

At the same time, I notice Zandolee from the corner of my eye. Zandolee wasn't really all there, if you know what I mean. He had a habit of pacing up and down the street. Sometimes he woulda just stand like a gunslinger in front of the street sign, playing with his dreads and whistling 'Three Little Birds'. Sam always liked to point him out to me whenever I wasn't doing my schoolwork. *You want to turn out like Zandolee over there?* he'd say to me.

Zandolee locked eyes with me and in that moment, I welled up with guilt and reconsidered going up to the farm. I thought about Sam. Sam was accustom to Nick lying to him. Not me. He had a lot of faith in me still. He still had some pride in me, tucked away somewhere in a corner of his mind. Zandolee finally looked away, I felt like somebody was always watching. Always listening. Not that Zandolee would be the one to sell me out. But I remembered that I was putting a lot on the table tonight.

Didn't take long for Raja and his Ford Fiesta to swoop by to get Nick. When they was gone, I set off.

As I pedalled past the crossroads and the samaan tree, a screech fly in from the distance, making me dig my nails into the brake handles. I stopped, taking a moment to breathe, gazing up at the starless sky. Something whisked right past me, cutting through the air. It nearly threw me off my bike. It went whipping in the wind, flapping into the trees. It was a bat, long like my arm.

At that moment, I considered turning around, riding right back home. I closed my eyes, leaned forward on the bike, taking in the slow creak of the chain crawling along the spokes. The low rumbling of the ravine from behind the trees. Crickets chirping.

Cicadas revving up. I told myself right then: I had to do it. I woulda rather regret doing something than doing nothing. So I started pedalling again. I didn't look back after that.

When I passed the mud-spattered track, I knew I was getting close because the wind started to carry that chicken stench. Two long patches of sun-dried bushes that spouted past my neck flanked the path. Just a minute of walking again and I finally spotted the farmhouse in the distance. I pushed the bike into a thick bush and hid it there. I started wading through the tall patchworks of grass, my arms moving in careful breaststrokes through them. I remember thinking at the time that I shoulda worn something with sleeves—the grass was like razorblades against my skin.

At the end of the thicket was a tatty wire fence that looped around the farmhouse grounds. The entrance gate was reinforced with a fat iron padlock. Clucking spilled out through the barbwire that was barricading the coops. It ain't even sound like chickens after a while—it just blended together like people haggling at the market.

A blue, paint-weathered pickup was park up near the shed. It was stacked with battery cages. There was two bikes lain against the side-gate, which was left ajar.

I approached the fence, keeping a steady lookout for Mangeshkar the Castrator. Just because I had no balls to bite off ain't mean I was invulnerable.

A loud crowing shot from the sheds. A screeching uproar from the other fowls followed. I drop down in a squat, staying like that for a while. Even after the noise settled, I was too nervous to move. It took me a while to muster up the courage to dash through the side-gate.

The farmhouse lights were on. The house was smaller than I expected. It was more of a shack. It was elevated a few feet on some concrete pillars, forming a small, dusty recess below, gutter pipes sloping down the galvanize roof, leading right down to two rainwater barrels. Behind the house was an overgrown cow-itch bush, a small scummy pond, and a shed that looked like it coulda be a pit latrine.

I scuttled towards the house. The door was open—I coulda see inside. By the time I entered, my heart was already beating fast-fast.

Three rooms. I counted it. To the front, a stove with a dining table and a busted TV. A dim filament bulb hung from a coiled wire at the top of the front room. Moths clicking against the bulb formed splotchy shadows on the wall. A kettle on the stove. Hunting knives hanging on the wall, coated with soap scum. Two horseflies tracing the rim of a corned beef tin on the table. Two plates set by the sink, each with scraps of breadcrust. No ceiling, just parallel wooden beams connected by spiderwebs.

I headed to the back where there were two small beds and a dresser. I pulled the top drawer. Just some old jerseys and sheets. The bloody crocus bag was nowhere to be seen. I dunno what else I was looking for. But I was looking. A scrap of a dress. A ribbon, shoe, earring, anything. I kept pulling drawers. In the last one, I saw something poking out from under some rags. I shifted them to the side.

It was a gun, big like my foot. I shut the drawer quick.

A man's voice came from outside. He was shouting. I crouch behind the dresser before slinking back to the kitchen area. From there I coulda tell that the shouts was coming from the coops. The man sounded like he had hot shale in his lungs. There was other voices, too. I couldn't make out the words but with each shout, the fowls was going crazy.

As I went outside and crept to the back, I nearly screamed. I clamped my hands over my mouth. Three huge skinned mongooses was strung up on a line. The rodents was gum-pink and twirling dead-slow like rotisseries on a skewer. Their eyes was gouge out. The bloody crocus bag was on the ground, tucked away next to some bricks. I felt relieved and stupid at the same time, knowing I finally found out what was in the bag.

A scream rang out, washing away the relief I had. It sounded like a child. I made my way to the coops and peeped through a side-vent. The door was open on the other side and through it, I saw two fowls circling each other in the yard—an erminette and a brown leghorn. The two birds were in a circle scraped into the dirt, lined with stone.

The leghorn hoisted its wings. The erminette was scratching the dirt with its feet. Two metal spikes strap to its spurs. It kicked at the leghorn, slicing one of the spikes right through its wing. And the entire coop exploded again. There was about half a dozen people there, their backs to me. Lambi and Duster in their own corner. Lambi was leaning against an old broken concrete post, tracing his muddy slippers against the ground. Mangeshkar next to him wagging her tail. Duster was stooping down with his head below his shoulders, his dhal-stained shirt unbuttoned, exposing his scrawny chest and wrinkled paunch. The blue of his tattered jeans long wash away. His grey hair made a swirl near the bald spot of his crown. He scratched the greys that bristle his half-shaven face.

I pressed my palms along the boards, trying my best to catch a better view. There was some older men there—I didn't recognize them. One of them had a little boy, looking about eight years old. The child yelled out at the fowls, "Get 'im! Get 'im! Get 'im or you gonna get dead tonight!"

The erminette fowl kicked up some dust and made for another swipe. It missed.

Duster flung his arms up in the air, crying out, "I currying this blasted, no-good bird tomorrow! Dumb dodo bird!" He kicked the leghorn towards the coop, in my direction, and the child busted out laughing.

The leghorn saw me and began approaching me behind the coop. It twisted its neck, all its feathers spread-out like spines on a cactus. I jerked my nose at it, mouthing at it, *Go away! Go!*

Duster turned to the bird, squinting in my direction. Lambi unfolded his arms. Mangeshkar's ears went straight up.

Duster sprang to his feet, tilting his head to see around the coop. The fowl let out a noise that sounded like vomiting—flailing its wings as it made a kicking dash towards me, the spikes on its spurs grazing my leg.

I wasn't having none of it. I spin around and took right off.

That was when Duster bawl out, "You feel you could run?"

I looked behind me just to see Mangeshkar taking chase, kicking up a cloud of dirt. I pounce up to the gate, slam it and clicked the padlock as soon as I was on the other side. The dog launched at the gate, scrabbling its paws to get over it. She missed me by just a hair. I was on the other side of the gate, frozen, watching the dog readying herself for another bound. I didn't know if she could make it over and I wasn't sticking around to find out.

I kept running till I trip over some grass and nearly tumbled into a bush. Struggling crazier than a flipped turtle, trying to regain my bearings, the lights of the pickup shone hot on me. The growl of the engine blasted in the air. They get a good look at me then, I'm sure.

I raced down the muddy track, running straight past my bike and eventually breaking off from the path and into the backwoods. There was no time. *Klank!* I spun around to see the pickup slamming through the front gate. The pickup stammered over the sloping track, crashing down like thunder on its own weight. I was off at full speed, so fast that I wanted to vomit. I cut through a coppice and ended up at a ravine that separated the backwoods from the village.

Either that or I could go back on the road and risk being steamrolled. I made a mad sprint and leapt right across the ravine.

When I land, I skidded down the bank. I leaned all my weight forward, fluttering my arms to keep balance. I fell on the balls of my thumbs and clawed up the grime before scurrying up to the top and taking off again.

The pickup wasn't far. I coulda hear it. My street was too far away—but even if it was just a stone's throw away, there was no way I was going home. I woulda had to lose my mind to dock into that empty house. Tiki's house on Hallelujah Terrace was just seconds away.

CHAPTER 7

YOU THINK YOU TRYING TO PROTECT ME BUT YOU'RE NOT.

I made a wild gallop up to the front of Tiki's house and with a single cat leap, grappled onto the chain-link fence. I looked up and saw Tiki pull his curtains, as if he was expecting me. I landed square on the other side of the fence. Had to take a second to catch myself. I pulled myself up the toolshed, struggling to keep my footing.

Finally got to the back window where Tiki reached his hand down to pull me up.

As he did, I hear a *thud* from below me.

He jerked back. I gritted my teeth, turning to look down—my right sandal had slip off my foot and bounce right onto the galvanize. A grunt spill through from another room.

"What the hell goin on in there, boy?" It was Mr. Kangal.

Tiki gave my arm a sharp tug—so hard that I thought my shoulder was going to pop off. I kicked my feet upward and the other sandal went flying off. Once I was in the room, he shut the window, pulled the curtains, and shove me under the bed, prodding me into a corner with the side of his foot. He dive into bed, same speed.

There was a dead lizard under there. I dunno if I killed it or if it was already dead when I got there.

Heard the door open. Then a click—and the room was drowning with light.

"Blasted cat and them causin a damn ruckus this hour of the night. Shoulda poison them long time," Mr. Kangal's voice rumbled sleepily as he pace towards the window. After a molasses-slow minute, the old man shut the window, sucking his teeth. He closed the drapes and left the room, switching the light off and shutting the door behind him.

"He gone," Tiki whispered, giving the side of the bed a small tap.

"It safe?"

"I just say he gone."

I crawled out and sat on the floor, grabbing my knees and squeezing them hard. "Have a dead lizard under there, you know that?"

"Be quiet, or two of we gonna be two dead lizards." He paused. "The old man ain't right today. Is since mornin he sit down with the bottle."

"Just gimme a minute," I tell him. "I'll be outta your skin when I know Duster's gone."

His jaw dropped and he threw the sheets off of him "You outta your mind?" he hiss out. "You and these brain-dead schemes!"

"You mean hare-brain?"

"No, I mean brain-dead!"

Just then, a voice boomed from the street and my stomach went sour like tamarind.

Tiki parted the drapes so fast that he nearly tear the curtains off. "You let them jumbies follow you way out here!" He was frantic, his cheeks all puffed up. "Bring the Horsemen of the Apocalypse too, one time!"

Duster shouted out, "Lil hooligan fowl t'ief! I know you in there!"

I clenched my teeth. I didn't want to go to the window but I had to. All the dogs in the street was barking. One by one, the neighbours' lights came on.

Duster scooped up a stone from the road and—

"Duck!" I gasped.

The stone came flying right through the front window—it hit the floor, *bop!*

I peeked out again just as Duster picked up another stone to hurl at the house. It hit the roof before swivelling down the side of the gutter pipe.

Mowww. Mr. Kangal growling from the other room.

"Quick!" Tiki hiss, grabbing my arm. He shove me under the

bed again.

The door creaked open and Mr. Kangal lurched into the room, grumbling, "Boy, what the hell goin on here?"

"Someone stoning the house," Tiki said.

Mr. Kangal clamp his palms down on the windowsill and called out, "Who that there? Don't make me cuff down y'old ass, eh! The hell you doin, peltin my house!"

At the same time, Duster yell back, "You better count yuh blessings, knowin I ain't bring mi glock here wit me, fowl t'ief!"

"Who you callin t'ief?" Mr. Kangal shot back.

Clang! It sounded like Duster hit the guttering this time. "Man, you send yuh imp child to t'ief mi birds!"

"Aye, you old dog! My boy here in bed sleepin!"

"Boy? I ain't talkin bout no boy! The girl chile!"

Mr. Kangal turned to Tiki. "I ain't have no girl chile, senile fool!" As soon as he finished his sentence, he pulled away from the window. Looming over the bed now, he asked, "You know something that I don't?"

Tiki, sounding like he was ready to piss his pants, couldn't come up with nothing except, "He talkin nonsense, Pa."

"Mister man," the old man said, "you will get me vex this hour—"

"Is nonsense, Pa."

"I goin down these stairs to see what this jackass really want from me," Mr. Kangal said. "You stay here if you know what good for you!"

As soon as he was gone, I slithered out from under the bed and dusted myself off. Tiki had this pouting, tired look.

I knelt down at the bedside, pressing my elbows and chin against the mattress as if I was going to pray. Maybe I shoulda been praying, I thought. None of this was fair to Tiki. I had gotten him involve in something he wanted no part of. It wasn't fair to him and

I didn't want Mr. Kangal to catch me in here—not in the state he was in. Not in the state everything was in. I shoulda never come here, I told myself. "I'm gonna make a run for it," I tell him.

"What you mean, make a run for it? Run where? They right outside!"

"I could get out through the back fence. They won't see me."

He crane his neck at me. "Rune, that is the recipe for gettin caught."

"If they catch me, best they catch me out there, not in here. I don't want you getting in trouble over my foolishness."

"You think you trying to protect me but you're not." He was pleading now. "Stay here and let it blow over. What? You think he going to check under the bed?"

He reached over and grabbed my wrist, but I broke away.

I went to the back window and hopped one leg over the sill. Same time, I saw my sandal on the galvanize below me. I stretched my toes, careful not to rattle it. I slipped the sandal back on, keeping on the lookout for the other. Getting up the tool-shed was never a problem. Two strong hoists and I could be up in ten seconds flat. Getting down was the scary part. A pair of wooden poles bolstered the shed. I latched onto one and slid down, my hands burning from the friction.

I skittered down to the water tank and squatted in its shadow. One hand on my knees and the other pressing against the structure. Seconds felt like minutes. I pinched some of the moss off my fingers. The candleflies was hovering around a cluster of ixoras. There, I saw my other sandal. I just had to stretch myself to get it.

I reached for it, stretching till I thought my spine would pop out from my pelvis. And I finally got it. As soon as I turned around to go back—*sssssssss!*

I fell over, my hand slapping against a tuft of fur. Two yellow eyes glared back at me. The cat jolted back, tail pointing straight up, back arching.

Sssssss! It bared all its teeth to me.

I moved to swat it away, but not before it took a swipe at my wrist, drawing three thin lines of blood from it. I let out a loud yelp as the cat launched itself back into the darkness.

Immediately, my eyes flick over to the two old men. They turned their eyes to me and Mr. Kangal started approaching, taking slow steps towards the tank. Each step, I felt like a hot metal ball was getting bigger and bigger in my guts.

I held my breath until he was close enough to see me. When our eyes connected, I thought of just running off. I thought of kicking him in the balls. But I just stood up and walked into the light. I thought of Tiki, feeling that pang of guilt hit me again right in the belly. Running wasn't gonna solve nothing. My feet knew it. My muscles knew it. There was nowhere to run. Nowhere to hide. It was already over and I felt the same way I felt when I saw the mongooses—equal parts stupid and relieved.

CHAPTER 8

YOU THINK IT MATTERS WHAT I OR ANYBODY ELSE THINK?

Nobody was sure who call the police. The police car pull up only seconds after Duster and Mr. Kangal marched me out onto the sidewalk like I was to be executed by firing squad or something. Duster's fingers was still latching onto my shoulder, his nails sharp like parrot talons.

The constable came out, arms akimbo, eyes sharp on me. His grey, double-pocket uniform was starched and clean. Almost city-boy clean. He ain't look like an officer of the law so much. He looked like he coulda be a primary school teacher. I pictured him before a stack of books, helping children out with their times tables. Still, I couldn't keep my eyes off the gun strap to his waist. Some of the neighbours was watching from their windows. Looking back on it, this was when I started to feel like this whole thing was real. The constable introduced himself as PC Arjuna.

"What you doing out so late, young lady?" he asked, half-stooping before me. He then turned to Duster and Mr. Kangal. "Got a call about a disturbance. We have a disturbance?"

Duster scoff at the constable and spat out, "The young lady here is a disturbance. Drag this vermin down to the station and make a example outta she, y'hear?"

"Tell me what she did."

"She is a t'ief!"

"Thief? What she thief?" Arjuna asked. He then looked at me, "What you thief?"

"Fowl t'ief, she is!" Duster said. "She was on mi property, tellin you!"

"Fowl? What you was going to do with these fowls?" Arjuna asked me, his tone unusually playful. "Fry? Honey barbecue?" I had a feeling like this wasn't the first time he was dealing with Duster.

"Everything is a blasted joke to these police," Duster muttered to Mr. Kangal, sucking his teeth.

The constable looked straight at Mr. Kangal. "You know,

chicken larceny gettin the death penalty soon. And this young lady here gonna be the first in line at the hangman." He put his palm on my shoulder. "The trespassing, on the other hand—well, that one ain't no joke." He stood up straight, tone more serious now. "Damn sure you wouldn't want to wake up one night and find old Duster here creepin round in your backyard, mmm?"

I locked eyes with the constable for the first time, taking comfort in the fact that this man had more authority than them other two. He led me to the backseat of the squad car. Duster was fuming now. "You ain't gonna slap the cuffs on she?"

"Don't think it have a need to."

"Tellin you, this one sneaky!"

"She don't pose no danger to me. She pose a danger to you?"

"Bah! Waste of time police!"

As Arjuna shut the door, he kept his palm against the glass and added, "If you could promise me some kinda headline tomorrow not gonna have PC Arjuna handcuffing a little girl, then yeah, I'd consider it. So I prefer take the sane route here. You ain't the one paying the rent, uncle."

Mr. Kangal took a slow step back from Duster, scratching the back of his head, shame now setting in. Maybe he was beginning to sober up. It was one of the few times I had seen him admit wrong— even though it wasn't said out loud. All of that woulda be all for naught once he got time to sit down with the bottle again, though. I looked out the car window up at Tiki's room. The window was shut, the drapes closed. I don't think anybody realized I was up there, so I was thankful for that. I did the right thing.

Arjuna looked at me through the rearview. He asked for my name, full name.

"Arundhati Mathura," I tell him. Then adding, "People round here just call me Rune."

"Think we need to go down to the station, Ms. Mathura?"

"I ain't think so."

"Good. Me neither. So, let's just get you home safe, Ms. Mathura. You live near here?"

"Shepherd Street."

"That's right there. You coulda walk there but now your parents gonna have to see you pulling up in a squad car. What they gonna think when they see that?"

I paused then told him, "Nobody home."

He looked at me through the rearview again, furrowing his brow. "Where are they?"

"I live with my grampa."

"Where grampa at?"

"At a wake." Then I added, "My brother suppose to stay home with me."

"Older?"

"Yeah."

"So where brotherman at?"

"Can't say for sure."

He raised his eyebrows.

"Maybe you could try Flambeau," I tell him.

"Flambeau? What he doing there?"

"Drinking." I took a while to answer.

He let out a heavy sigh. "Mmm, look like we making a station trip after all."

On the ride there, I tried to go over the whole night in my head. Tried to justify it, tell myself I did what nobody else woulda do. That I do the right thing tonight, no matter the consequences. And it come to mind, how come chicken become a slang for coward? For sure now, after tonight, I know not all of them ain't cowards. I think when they saying that, they're talking about the majority. The ones in coops and battery cages all their lives, bred to await no other endgame and treatment but slaughter.

Chickens know they gonna die. Because when they see the hands coming for them, they all cluck and flail into a corner till one of them is snatch up. As soon as that door open, they know it's time. Then five minutes later, they go back to pecking the dirt. That's kinda like how we are sometimes. We make noise and shut ourself off in a corner when one of our own is killed. Then we go back to pecking once the blood is hosed off. There's so many of them and they can't come together. They can't plan, they can't conspire. They just know: the door opens, the hand swoops down, grabs one, the door closes and the rest of us are safe for a few hours.

We can tell the trend. We can plan ahead. We can be smart about it. But we follow the same pattern: door open, hand, grab, door close, safe. Because, like the chickens, there might be the one rogue who jabs at the hand and they're the one who's gonna get pluck out of the flock first. It don't make a lick of sense to be the one lean, mean, fighting-machine fowl if everybody else already gone back to pecking the ground. No matter how big and bad and scary you is, you'd just look like a fool running towards the slaughter.

When we got there, he walked me to the front desk and quickly scribbled out a form. An older man behind the desk glanced at me, shaking his head before he went back to watching the cricket highlights on his portable TV. I had never been in no police station before and I know it was late at night, but I wasn't expecting it to be so lifeless. I was expecting notice boards crowded with bulletins and wanted posters and criminal sketches. An officer on the phone issuing an APB. I felt a little stupid that I was expecting those things. Everything was rundown. The termite-bitten desks look like they coulda collapse under the weight of all the manila folders bloated with dog-eared documents. The officers at the desks paid me no mind. There was only about four of them, each with their own slice of paperwork. One of the officers stood near the louvres, a half-smoked cigarette in his mouth. Next to him was an empty desk.

Arjuna prattled off some instructions to the desk officer so fast I wasn't even sure it was English. He took me to a lady officer and handed her the form. "Navarro, babysit this one for me."

She rolled her eyes at him. "Seriously?"

"Her brother coming to pick her up soon." Before she could say anything, he said, "You're a saviour, Navarro!" And then he was gone.

Constable Navarro was young, looked like she was in her early thirties. Her hair was tie up in a bun, with some stray curls falling over her temples. Her navy blue uniform and waist-belt was struggling to keep her figure in. She looked mixed—maybe with Venezuelan. She was humming along to Richard Marx's 'Right Here Waiting' on the radio as she read through the form. She copy the information into another document. I was watching her write. She had a nice fountain pen.

"You're going to get yourself shot going into other people's property like that," she said, her eyes still on the forms.

I wasn't going to say anything till she raised her eyes at me. I told her, "I had my reasons."

"I'm sure you did," she said, putting the pen down, her elbow against the desk, cheek cradled in her palm. "I'm curious about those reasons though."

I wasn't going to lie to no officer. I was already in enough trouble. "I had a feeling."

"A feeling? About what?"

"I saw the son with a bloody bag. He was carrying it into the house."

She crinkle her brow. "Bloody bag? How'd you manage to see this?"

"Um, I just happen to see it," I said, rubbing my nose.

"You're his neighbour?" She picked up her pen again.

"No. I was just there."

"But not randomly." She pointed the pen at me. "You were spying on the son."

"Not spying." She smirked as if she knew I woulda get offended by the word.

"Investigating then?"

"Yeah. That's a better word."

"You found out what was in the bag?"

"I dunno. I think it was mongoose."

"A-ha, well, mystery solved." She was sitting up straight now. "But we have another mystery—why were you investigating the boy?"

I was torn at this point. I remembered the old lady at the Chinese restaurant who got her throat slit three times. I knew the constable was going to listen—and I felt like I desperately needed somebody who was willing to do that. So I told her the truth, "Dumpling."

She crinkle her brow. "Dumpling?"

"Um, Devi Heera," I say, rubbing my nose. "The girl they find buried near the river. In class, we used to call her Dumpling."

"So you think this fella had something to do with it?"

"Something about him give me a bad feeling. I think he coulda do it."

"Do what? Kill and bury that girl?"

"It's a feeling."

"That is a hell of a feeling to have." She nodded, eyes tilted to the ceiling. "So we have a Nancy Drew here."

I was annoyed by her demeaning tone. "Jessica Fletcher," I said, trying to sound smart.

"What?"

"*Murder, She Wrote.*"

"Right, yeah." She let out a big laugh. I wasn't sure if she was laughing at me or in general. Either way, I was annoyed and I regretted telling her anything at that moment. "So you thought the chicken farmers killed your classmate? For what reason?"

I hesitated. "Not Duster. Just Lambi."

"Right. Why?"

"It don't matter now anyway."

"Sounds like you just didn't like the boy."

I shrugged. "You don't think he coulda do it?"

"You think it matters what I or anybody else think?" She went back to writing. "No secret those two have a bit of a funny history. But that's not enough to accuse them of anything. All that matters is the evidence."

"So the police investigate them? I ain't see anything like that in the news."

"Not all police work is shown on the news, you know. The investigation is still pending, so I can't tell you the straight details—but don't you think they'd be the first people to investigate?"

"And you ain't find any evidence—"

"Pending."

"Sorry." I retreated into myself a little, staring down at my feet. "What about the bitemark?"

She stopped writing, set her pen down and looked right at me, her mouth frozen in an O. "Where—" she began but stopped herself, craning her neck. "Jessica Fletcher is really good at tracking down killers, isn't she?"

I mean, I agreed. But I didn't know what kinda response she wanted. So I just nodded.

She just looked at me, shaking her head. "You're no Jessica Fletcher." She observed me for a few seconds, my confused expression. Then said, "Bet you're wondering why I said that. It's one of my favourite shows too. There's this early episode where Jessica tells this man that he might end up a character in the book. He asks if he's going to be the killer in the book. And Jessica just says: *I haven't made up my mind yet.* That's how a real detective would act. You know what was the difference between you and Jessica Fletcher tonight?"

It took me a few seconds but when it hit me, it hit me. And I couldn't feel more stupid. I turned my eyes to the floor. "I already made up my mind who was the killer."

"See, you aren't so dumb after all. Unless you have the evidence, everything is a possibility." She fiddled with the pen, flicking it between her fingers. Deep in thought, quiet for a while. She edged closer to me. "What you did tonight was incredibly stupid, but I understand what you're trying to do. I know it's coming from somewhere that I can't possibly know. But I understand it. I'm not telling you not to do it but you have to be smarter about it."

I bowed my head. "Yeah." I didn't regret talking to her. I felt like it was something I needed, for someone to just be straight with me. No beating around the bush. Just someone to level me.

"Lemme tell you a story," she said. "There was this big starch mango tree near my house when I was small. Anytime I set out to climb it, there was always a woman passing by to yell at me and tell me to get down. Then she'd ask me, *Child, why you leaving your poor mother to do all the housework?* I'm not even sure if this woman even knew my mother. She certainly didn't know me."

"So what happen?"

"Never made it to the top. Then it became impossible."

"Impossible how?"

"Well, one day they cut down the tree."

"Because you wanted to climb it?"

"No. Because the tree was diseased. Trunk rot fungus spreading up to the branches. It was decaying from the inside. I'm not saying the old woman was right. But I literally would've been climbing up the wrong tree."

Before I could respond, she added, "Could've broken my leg."

She turned to me again. I had my eyes on the floor. "You could break much more if you keep climbing this tree. But if you really want to make a difference—come back here when you turn eighteen and you're a little bit taller. There could be a spot for you." My gaze drifted to the officer blowing his cigarette smoke through the louvres, then back to the heap of paperwork on Navarro's desk. I reminded myself that it was all a tedious process and this wasn't TV. You couldn't put the real thing on TV. It had to be a gradual thing.

An older moustached officer came up to the desk. He said to Navarro, pointing at the door, "The brother's here." Navarro tipped her chin at the officer. She then gave me a little nod before going back to her work.

CHAPTER 9

GREEN TAILS AND LEGS AND HEADS. A HEAP OF THEM.

"Thanks for shitting up the night," Raja said to me as he turned the corner to veer into the main road. He had that corny 'I'm Too Sexy' song pounding from the radio.

Through the rear view, he shot a look at Nick, who was sitting slumped over next to me. As soon as I get in the car, I smell the alcohol on his breath. Even Raja's *Eternity for Men* couldn't drown out the stench. Raja was the one to claim me at the station.

"Just drop the girl home. She is a big girl," Nick was slurring. This was also why him being sober made me nervous—because the next time he'd get drunk, he'd get drunk enough for five people, ready to piss the life outta him. I was mad, but I wasn't in no position to talk right now.

Raja suck his teeth. "How we could drop the girl home and nobody there, eh?" He looked at me through the rear view. "How the hell you think she get herself into this shit in the first place?"

"I just need one more and we could call it a night," Nick asked. "The night need to end proper."

I could tell Raja didn't want to argue. As he pulled up in front of Flambeau, he tell Nick, "We can't leave the girl in the car alone. You think Gaudy would mind?" I didn't want to go but I didn't protest.

"Gaudy is a good man. Is just a lil in-and-out we goin for," Nick said, putting on his shades.

"Take off them ridiculous things," Raja snap at him. "You look like an asshole, driving away all the girls."

Nick grinned. "Aye, never mess with a guy in shades, eh."

"We sitting outside," Raja said. "So Gaudy can't say nothin."

In the road near the car park was Salaman's Roadster. Then I saw Salaman himself at the bar. I half-expected him to be sweeping but he was just there, having a beer by himself. There was at least twenty patrons at the tables lain out across the small wood scaffolding outside the bar, and a dozen boozing at the counter. Gaudy, the owner, always lined the front windows every night with all the top brands—Carib, Stag, Stout, Heineken—brimming with kerosene, topped with burning cloth scarves. The wind swayed the flames like broomstick skirts, matching the groove of 'Bacchanal Lady'.

Flambeau was along a lonely stretch of road, not far from the village. Still, business was always booming. It help that it was next to a bridge, where the cars always had to slow. Beneath the bridge was a wide ravine that flowed along the side of the bar. At the end of every week, Gaudy had to wade down there himself to fish out the bottles that rolled down the bank.

Raja got us a table outside. It was noisy. Three men at a nearby table was quarrelling about Abu Bakr and the coup, and how much better it was when the Federation was around. Another crew went on and on about cricket, slamming down their fists with each mention of Lara and Tendulkar. Two heavyset men clicking billiard balls while the dings of a slot machine cut into the conversations. A TV sat in a cage at the corner of the ceiling. *Predator* was showing, bullets biting the leaves as Arnold Schwarzenegger fired round after round into the jungle.

I sat down watching a young woman in a red scooter-skirt dancing by herself near an empty bar stool. Her long hair bobbing in a wild tumble of dyed brown curls. Every once in a while, she took a swig of Carib and twirl her skirt. She was very pretty. Sleek nose, big pouting lips—the kind of pretty that could get a man in trouble. Her face was so drench with foundation that her face looked a totally different complexion from her neck. Her eyes were flitting about the room. Looking to see who was watching. She remind me of a raccoon, the amount of mascara and kajal she had caked on.

Nick was leering at her. "Look your girlfriend here," he

uttered to Raja.

Rita—or *force-ripe Rita* as the women used to call her. She had breasts since she was nine. She woulda be about eighteen or nineteen then. She went to school with Nick and Raja. Boys used to pay her their lunch money to see her chest, Nick say. I never bothered to ask if he was one of them boys. I know Raja was. I think that's how he had fall in love with the girl. Who knows? He probably pay her to stop showing her chest to other boys.

They wasn't together no more, but a few years back they was the real deal. Rita and Raja. Everybody used to ask them to be invited to the maticoor. He was saving up for a ring and all. Nick used to talk about them all the time. I think he was a little jealous. The way he used to talk, you woulda swear he had a thing for Rita. Maybe he did.

Raja and Rita didn't need no big bad wolf to send the house tumbling down, though. Everybody in Kukuyo know the stories— Raja woulda go on and on about all the clothes he buy for her. How she pile them up and set them on fire in the backyard. And how he used to bawl up at her in public, telling her to stop talking so much, how she was always making herself sound so *uneducated*. He broke it off after he catch her in the toilet, cutting the white horse with a razor, a dollar bill ready to sniff it all up. That was the last straw. I dunno how many people knew that. I only knew because Nick knew.

"Shit," Raja muttered out. "She come outta nowhere. She was hiding in a hole this whole time?"

"Well, she working hard. Getting clients."

Raja looked at him. "What you mean?"

At the same time, Gaudy hauled himself to our table, eyes on us like lasers. The throbbing veins on his scalp was on clear display. A hairy curve of belly-flesh droop from under his black Henley shirt. Though no patron ever see the man lick a drop of his own medicine, his eyes was always as swollen and yellow as a seasoned rumcork.

"Fellas, fellas. This is plain-as-day disrespect," he said.

"Gaudy, don't make no trouble," Nick said.

Gaudy whipped Nick's shades right from his face, dangling them between his fingers.

Nick slouched forward. "That is how you be treatin your number one customers, Gaudy?" he said, tracing his finger over the soot in the ashtray.

Gaudy pointed a rigid finger at me, grunting, "This girl is no customer of mine, boy. Get it straight." He didn't look away from Nick. "I let you fellas come in my establishment, take your drinks, have your fun. You could pass for legal—good with me. But I give you an inch and now you taking a mile."

Raja gave Gaudy a gentle tap on the wrist and, with astonishing ease, retrieved the shades from Gaudy's grip. He didn't hand them back to Nick till Nick gestured for them.

"We ain't here to cause no trouble. You feel we stupid? The girl ain't drinkin," Raja said and slammed a twenty down on the table. "Two Heinekens and we outta your skin. You could keep the change."

Gaudy twisted his mouth at us. He swiped the money off the table and pointed at Nick, "I am a respectful man. And I respect Sam. And if Sam come down here, talkin bout this—"

"Sam ain't talkin bout shit because Sam ain't gonna find out shit," Nick said, turning to me. "Right?"

"Right," I said. It was going to be Nick's ass if Sam found out Nick brought me to Flambeau. I was wondering if Nick realized that or if he just didn't care no more.

Gaudy left to get the beers. As he left, Raja asked again, "What you mean, getting clients?"

"You ain't hear?" Nick said, grinning.

"Hear what? You trying to get me vex, Nick?"

"She hustling now."

"Hustling? What you mean?"

"I dunno. Some guesthouse not too far from here. Sunflower or something."

"What the hell you mean, hustling?" Raja lean in on him. "You mean, like—"

"She giving it up for money."

"Wait, you mean is Sundew she gone and shack up in? Is only the grime of the earth does go there. What she doin there? How the hell you know this?"

"I hear one of them men talking about it. No shame, he say he pay for a half hour. You couldn't even pay me to do—"

"One of them men? Who exactly is one of them men?" Raja slumped back in his chair, his chest heaving with each breath.

"It matter?" Nick chuckled. But when Raja glared at him, he spill it out, "Omar from the construction site, boy. You know how the man nasty already—"

"Omar?" Raja spit out. "You mean Omar who shack up with Gonorrhoea Gayatri and braggin how she so good that everything still burnin and leaking for days after?" Raja's head looked like it was about to explode. "How much people she do this with?"

"I dunno, Raja."

"Gimme a number, Nick."

"Hold up. Lemme check my ledger for the inventory," Nick said, pretending to open a book. Raja wasn't amused. Nick then said, "She probably cheap. Cheaper than the putas who coming down from Caracas. You could get a D-cup Indian in any chutney fete for free so I doubt she charging much. She ain't exactly too sane either, but even you didn't care bout that—"

"You could shut up now, Nick," Raja grunt, his hands clasped over his head.

Was hard to believe Raja didn't know about Rita and Sundew. Sundew, well, you couldn't miss it. Was just two buildings down from the mandir and the barbershop. Wasn't no secret what use to go on there. Men used to get their haircut, do their puja and then shack up with one of the Venezuelans there. The man who ran there, he called himself Pan—as in Peter Pan. *Clap if you believe*, he does say, *because I could make men fly!*

Pan had video cameras in the walls and he used to get off on watching big men get it on with young girls. I felt sick the first time I hear that. I imagined the girls struggling to force a smile, a hairy belly rubbing up and down, the man grunting, *It feel good, eh? I does do it good, eh?*

Gaudy returned with the Heinekens. I didn't look at him but I know he was eyeing me. He said to Nick, "The customer ain't always right, y'hear, boy? Git your tail outta here when that drink finish."

Nick brushed him off. "When the drink finish, my tail outta here," he said, taking a very slow sip of the beer. Gaudy suck his teeth and went back to the counter.

Nick's eyes was on Rita the whole time. Mine too. The empty barstool was now occupied by Salaman. He was wearing an old moth-chewed shirt jac, the sleeves blotted up with brown—blood from dead mosquitoes. Rita brushed her palm against the side of his beard as if she was petting a horse's mane. She leaned towards him, tapping his chin with her finger, and tilted a beer bottle against his lips. She spilled a little on his beard and wiped it up with a napkin.

"This is real—what I seeing here?" Raja's face was scrunch up like he swallow a bad oyster. Nick couldn't stop staring. His expression—half-amusement, half-horror. Raja pounded his fist against the table. "She might as well do it with a dog! Like an actual pothound!"

Nick gave him a smirk. "Maybe she did."

At the same time, Salaman smack his lips and pulled out a

roll of twenties from his pocket. Rita guided his hand back to his trousers. He grinned again, his bulbous nose flaring. Still holding his hand, Rita took the lead as they strolled out of the bar and across the gathering of tables outside.

"Jamette!" Raja called out, feigning a cough as she brush past our table.

She stopped, taking a long, hard look at the three of us.

Salaman looked too. He was looking right at me. His hands was in his pocket, making this clinking sound like he was jingling loose change. He crack a smile at us. I wasn't sure if it was at me or Raja. I ain't never seen Salaman smile till that night. And it catch my eye—because he was missing three upper teeth. His lower canines stuck out like a bulldog's.

His face looked fractured when he smiled. He opened his mouth like a fish would, gums pink like the inside of a conch shell. And he wiggle his tongue at us—but his eyes was on me while he was doing it. I felt queasy after that.

Rita grabbed his hand and stormed off with him.

Right after, Raja noticed Gaudy behind us shaking his head. Raja said to the man, "You know what she doin now, right?"

Gaudy shrugged. "That ain't concern me."

Raja raised his eyebrows at him. "It ain't concern you that it have some jamette in here spreading disease to your customers?"

Nick added, "It have limits, Gaudy."

"She doin she business, and I doin mine. Once she ain't bringin trouble, I don't care. Choose your women wisely next time, man. Who tell you to bring Jean and Dinah, Rosita and Clemontina home to mammy, eh?"

Nick bust out laughing. Raja, however, was too busy glaring down Rita to even acknowledge him. He wedged the beer between his lips so hard that the bottleneck clink against his teeth. He muttered out, "She doing this to make a fool outta me, you know."

"I telling you a long time now that she ain't worth it. The girl is damaged goods. All the warning signs was clear as day. Remember the lizard?" Nick looked at me. "You know the story bout the lizard, Rune?"

I looked at him funny. "Lizard?"

Nick threw a look at Raja who had this distant look in his eyes. "I could tell her?"

I wasn't sure if I wanted to hear it, but Raja flip his hand, giving him the go-ahead.

Nick began the story: "She wasn't long outta school when it happen. They put she to mow the lawn. So, she there mowing the lawn and then she hear, *scraaak!* She run over something. When she gone to move the lawn mower, is tails she seeing. Green tails and legs and heads. A heap of them. Is a family of lizards she run over!"

I cringed as he busted out laughing. I didn't even know what to say or think.

He continued, "The gal went half-mad. Nearly dead from fright. Run up and down the road screaming for every man and he mother to hear."

"A lizard would give the bitch a heart attack," Raja said, sipping his beer.

Nick carried on, "One time she went to eat dinner over at Raja house. Was around Christmas. I remember we was all at the table eating when she just fling a plate of food in the air. Pastelles and all." Raja was shaking his head the whole time. "You know why? Somebody had the TV on and—Raja, tell her what was showing."

Raja put his head down. "The girl ain't want to hear this, Nick."

"Tell her!"

I put my head down too. "*Godzilla,*" Raja said, shaking his head.

Nick busted out laughing. Was like he was forcing it now. He stopped, clearing his throat when he realized he was the only one. He said, "Well, hopefully it have none of that over at Sunshine—"

"Sundew," I corrected him, rolling my eyes. I got up. I was getting fed up. "I going back and wait by the car."

Nick flicked his hand, signalling for me to go ahead. "Stay right where I could see you, you hear?"

I walked off before he could finish his sentence. I waded through the crowd. A drunk man was blocking the ramp that descended from the scaffolding. He was sending kisses to a woman two tables away, hollering, *Family, family!* I didn't have no more patience. I elbowed past him and made my way back to the car.

I sat on the ground, my back to the tyres. Two stray dogs was making their mark on the front wheels. My head was throbbing. As I replayed the night in my mind, my eyes drifted to the steel-grey Toyota Cressida parked two cars down. 'Love is a Funny Feeling' jamming from the backseat speakers. The girls inside were laughing and passing around a bottle of cheap vodka. "Shit," I muttered out when I realized who they was. Alma and Krissy—here with a couple of older boys. The older boys had cigarettes tucked behind their ears. I don't think they notice me.

Watching Alma it was hard to believe we was the same age. I mean, I was seeing Alma around Kukuyo since we was small. Believe it or not, she used to be a quiet child. We never spoke, mainly because she was from the shantytown. I used to think the people there had some kinda mental disease, the way they was always cussing and brawling. People used to say all kinda things about the squatters. The one that I remember most was that the parents used to do it next to their children while they was sleeping. I dunno if it was true or not. Nasty things like that, people want it to be true so they could feel like they're better people.

Alma come with us to play jab-jab on Carnival Monday. It

was only the one time. She cut her mask out of Bristol board while we buy ours at the store. I think hers was suppose to be Medusa. We didn't know it was Alma at first. We didn't really know her enough to care either. We used to run over to Mitt's parlour with the jab-jab money and stock up on gummy bears and chocolates. I used to blow all of it on the *Bubble Bobble* machine. Alma used her money to buy a loaf of bread. I can't remember who it was that point it out and started laughing but we was all laughing eventually. I remember her looking right at me. To make it worse, I think this was around when her father had gone blind and couldn't work no more.

We didn't know none of that then, of course. That don't make it any less wrong. That we was small and stupid ain't make it any less wrong either. I don't think that was why Alma was how she was. There must've been a truckload of other things that I ain't even gonna pretend to understand. I couldn't say nothing, couldn't apologize. The damage was done already. I suppose we all have our things that make us feel like stains. I had mine. Alma had hers. I could bitch and complain how people write me off as darkskin and ugly but we was all guilty. We made up things about the squatters so Alma made up things about us. We called them names so she called us names.

I was going be Rune the Fowl Thief on Monday.

Rune the Hen Hunter. Rune the Rooster Robber.

I coulda just imagine it. Alma Reese pretending to be a chicken, elbows flapping up and down, going *bok-bok-bok*, scratching her shoes against the floor, calling out to me, *Cock-a-doodle-Ruuune!* I was already bracing myself for it.

A car pulled up to the side of the road in the distance, past the bridge. Buick Regal sedan, cream coat, mahogany brown roof. Joey Jodha's ride. He stepped out and lit a cigarette. He paced along the edge of the ravine, blowing rings of smoke over it. He was leaning on the abutment of the bridge, looking over at me. He flicked his cigarette into the water when he was done. As he crossed the bridge and got closer to me, the darkness wrapped around him. Because of the way he slouched, his silhouette looked headless—non-human. He looked at me sitting by the tyres but didn't acknowledge me. No faint look of recognition, nothing. Then he walked off.

About five minutes later, Raja dragged Nick back to the car.

Shepherd Street was only a short drive away. Still, they had to stop the car twice for Nick to vomit. When Raja finally pulled up to the house, he turned to me, grinning, "What you think Sam gonna do to you in the morning, girl? I coming over to see you get some licks."

Sam never beat me or Nick. We was lucky. Other people get it like crazy. Tiki, I remember he say his father would heat a kettle and dip the belt in hot water. Sam wasn't that kinda man. Instead, his voice used to go limp and scratchy with disbelief, sinking into disappointment. He either moped around the house all day or sat in his recliner, watching old Indian movies with this dead expression on his face. He had this one in particular he always put on called *Jai Santoshi Maa*. You knew you messed up if the *Jai Santoshi Maa* tape was out of its jacket.

Raja laughed. "When we use to get licks, we use to always make sure to wear an extra jeans to shield the blows." At the same time, Nick got down on his knees, hacking, vomiting right on the frontyard. Raja just sat there, watching. Nick's guts was flowing right outta him and Raja wouldn't even ask him if he was all right.

"If you talk to him, he mightn't drink so much." Took a lot outta me to be say it straight out with Raja.

Raja turned to me. "I tell him to drink?"

"Nick don't have no money. You the one buying all the drinks. So you the one calling the shots."

He didn't say nothing to that. There was no talking to him. He knew what he was doing a long time now. He was trying to make Nick dependent on him. I didn't have nothing else to say to Raja. I got out of the car and slam the door shut. Then I went to get my brother and carried him inside, making sure he didn't get vomit on his shoes.

APPETITE OF THE BEAST

CHAPTER 10

SORRY AIN'T GONNA CUT IT.

S am came home early the next morning. I heard the door open and the shower running. Then he got his things and went out again—probably to the market. Everybody know everybody in the market. So when Sam returned, the papers tuck under his arm, bag full of fruits and ground provisions, I knew that was it. He had to know what the hell went down.

I was watching from the window as he come up the street. As he approach the door, I slink back to the living room and sat on the hassock, heels pressed together, making sure to straighten up good. I remained like that, preparing myself for what was to come.

When he come in, he looked down at me, but ain't say a word. No good morning, nothing. He closed the door slow. Still facing it, he took a deep breath, set the papers and bag down on the counter and looked me direct in the eye.

Rubbing his bald crown, voice low and solemn. "Have anything to tell me, Anjali?"

My blood crawl, hearing him like that. A long afternoon was coming once Sam started calling me by my middle name—a name he told my mother to give me. "I raise you to steal?"

I couldn't keep my eyes on him. My gaze was bouncing all over the place. "I wasn't trying—"

"What business you had there?" he snap. I hesitate. I didn't even know where to start. But before I could say anything, he hiss out, "That Kangal boy went with you?"

"Tiki have nothing to do with it!" I was quick to retort on that one.

"One day, I goin to dead, y'know," he said. Letting out a sigh, his voice went glum with defeat. "The man you lookin at here, Anjali, is an old man." I began picking at my nails. I hated it—hearing him talk this way, about old age and death without a punchline.

He sat on the hassock next to me. "One day you goin to have

to decide how you want to be."

I couldn't do nothing but hang my head low.

"How you want to go down in this life. You want to go down as a thief? Fowl thief, of all things? Or you want to make good with what you have—and do good for others? We don't need no more low-class, garbage behaviour in this world."

I just nodded.

He continued, "Know what the final nightmare goin to be? I goin to meet your mother one day. When I get there, I gonna hafta look her in the eye and tell her that I leave her son drownin in a rum bottle. And that I let her daughter worm she way into a jail cell."

"They didn't put me in a jail—"

"You was damn close to it!"

My body jolt like a wasp sting me. Didn't have any words except, "Sorry."

He was shaking his head. "No. *Sorry* ain't goin to cut it. This one here, you ain't walkin away just so." He paused, looking at his shoes. "No, miss, you goin to have to learn bout crime and punishment. Me and you goin to have a talk with old Duster."

I cringed. Duster was the last person I wanted to see. But it was for the best. Didn't make sense being on the bad side of somebody like that. I forced myself to look Sam in the eyes and nodded. "I'll tell him I sorry."

"I say already, *sorry* ain't goin to cut it," he said, putting on his cap. "You goin to ask him for a job."

Sam didn't explain what he meant by *job* and I was feeling too guilty to ask. I didn't have no call here. Me and Sam tread up the track leading up to Duster's farm. I was trailing two or three steps behind him the whole time. As we pass the tall thickets of grass along the tract, I remembered that my BMX was still lodged in there. But I couldn't remember exactly where.

I reach my arm out, letting my palm sweep against the grass, feeling out for it, hoping my fingers would bump into a bicycle joint. But no luck. When we got to the end of the thicket, I wondered if Duster had already found it and sold it for scrap. It was on my mind to ask Sam to stop so we could look for it. He was the one who gave it to me after all. But as I motion to tug the old man's sleeve, I reminded myself that I was in no position to be asking for anything.

The farm looked strange in the daylight. Smaller, frailer. Two stray hens was clucking and scratching the ground near the shack. The skinned mongoose near the window was gone. Sam stood before the front gate.

He cupped his palms around his mouth and hollered out Duster's name.

No response. Not even from the hens.

Up till that moment, I was hoping the whole thing was a bluff. He called out again, louder this time. I hoped no answer would come.

But again, no luck. Duster come strolling in from the right, a sparse trail of chicken feathers behind him. A man about three times his size loom behind him, rummaging through a brown bag of salted nuts, grease staining his cheeks, belly bigger than any pregnant woman.

It looked like Duster recognize Sam because he was smiling at first. But his expression change when he spot me through the fence. "Them let that t'ief outta jail already!" He run up to the gate, eyeing me and Sam. "Sam, this is your people?"

"My one and only granddaughter."

"This t'ief? You makin me think less of you now, Sam."

Sam shook his head. "We here to make peace, boss."

Duster looked at him. "I make plenty t'ings in this life, pappy, but peace wit a t'ief?" He then looked right at me. "You know, in real countries a t'ief does get their hands chop off!"

The fat man hold his belly and started to laugh.

I looked up at Sam, hoping to see some sense prevailing in his face. But nothing, face still hard like stone. "Idle hands is the devil's playthings," Sam said. "I thinkin about puttin the girl to work."

Duster folded his arms and put his chin up like he already knew what was coming.

"What you say if the lil lady here could help out with a few things round the coops for a few days?" Sam said. The words creep outta his mouth as if he wanted to take them back. Even he knew this was foolishness. I didn't mind mowing a few lawns or helping a couple people out at the market. But it was only when Sam throw in the last part I knew he really lose it. "Free of charge."

I cringed. My mind cut back to the two chickens fighting, jabbing the metal spikes into each other. The pickup's lights blasting on me. The more I thought about everything, the guilt just dissolve away. Only to be replace by anger and frustration. And I started thinking, shit, Duster shoulda be the one apologizing to me!

Duster let out a belly laugh. "Granddaughter or not, Sam, I ain't lettin no t'ief on my farm. Me and the boy does manage good by weself anyway."

The fat man stepped up. "Baram Sirju. Sty Trail Farm." His voice was scratchy like sand. "T'ings getting kinda hectic down there right now. If Duster ain't taking up the offer, I can't let it go to waste."

"Sty Trail Farm? On Old Trunk Road?" Sam scratched his cheek. "You was selling ham last Christmas?"

Baram light up when Sam said that, face like a plum. "We known for we ham."

Duster folded his arms. "You lettin that t'ief in your property, Baram?"

Baram laughed. "Pigs too hard to t'ief."

"You never know. I could be the big bad wolf," I said. I couldn't sound more sour.

Sam gritted his teeth, but Baram was grinning wide like a crocodile. "I like wolfgirl here. I think me and she goin to get along good."

Sam's eyes were fixed on Baram, but I could see the nervousness in him—the way he was drumming his fingers against his hip. His eyes still on the man, he asked, "This man is a good man, Duster?"

"He ain't the Saviour," Duster said. "But I saying he have more to worry bout you than you have to worry bout he."

Sam reached his hand out to Baram. "Samardeep Mathura," he said.

Baram wiped his hands on his jersey. Sam's hand went limp at the end of the handshake. I suppose it was more of them *this gonna hurt me more than it hurt you* kinda deals. I couldn't help but feel like I was being sold off. I didn't think it woulda happen so easy. Baram looked at me, grinning again. "And wolfgirl's name here?"

"Arundhati," Sam said. He turned to me but his eyes was still on Baram. "She gonna give you a week's work." He turned to me. "You hear that? One week." I bite down on my lip.

Baram shrugged. "Once she can find she way down to the farm, we good to go."

"She have a bike. She can ride there," Sam said. "Morning time?"

Baram scratch the back of his neck. "Afternoon is when most of the melee does happen."

Sam clicked his tongue, raised his eyebrows at me. "After school then." I bite down on my lip to keep from cussing. School was enough of a headache already. Sam was asking me to jump outta the frying pan and into the fire here. The only saving grace was that it was just for one week. Maybe that's what he was telling himself too. He added, "I ain't want her coming home too late."

"I have a pickup. Could load the bike on there and get the girlie back home safe before dark."

"You ain't mind?"

Baram let out a laugh. "I ain't the one to mind, uncle." His gaze drifted to me. "I ain't the one workin for free." He gave Sam a flyer that he had in the back of his pickup. STY TRAIL FARM, big and bold, with a drawing of a pig mascot, a smirk on its face and a fork stuck into its backside. Under that, "COME PORK OUT!!!" If it was any other time, I woulda be laughing.

On the way back, Sam couldn't stop talking about pigs. How their hair was used for brushes and furniture, their skin for footballs, how the mother pigs sing to the nursing piglets. I didn't care. Sam coulda say anything—pigs was always going to be filthy creatures. I didn't say nothing to him. As soon as we get back to the house, I get myself up and march out the door. He ain't say nothing. I guess that was something to appreciate about Sam—if you was upset, he let you be upset. I guess he didn't want you saying things you woulda regret. Everything in its own time.

CHAPTER 11

AT LEAST YOU TRY.
YOU COULD SAY THAT.

Zandolee was pacing the street as usual. He stifle a snicker as I walk past him. People on the street was eyeing me down. Even the bread van man slow down to gawp at me. Can't lie and say it ain't bother me, but that was how people was. I come to accept it a long time now. I was already in hot water. I had to remember that I wasn't just Rune Mathura to these people. I was Sam's granddaughter. For his sake, I kept my trap shut whenever some old bat was watching me for too long.

I went over to Tiki's house. I told myself that I should use the front door this time—put on the sad eyes and apologize to the family. I still ain't think the whole thing was my fault, but I thought they at least deserved that. As I went up to the gate, I coulda hear the yelling. Mr. Kangal was drunk again. I often looked at Mr. Kangal when he was drunk and felt scared for Nick. For Mr. Kangal, it was like every time he drink, he was swallowing a ball of fire. And he had to bawl and holler to get it outta his stomach. Nick wasn't that kind of drunk. He just used to get tongue-tied and stupid and brave and happy. He wanted to love everything while Mr. Kangal wanted to hate, bash walls in, break doors down. His was more about anger than alcohol. About control.

Tiki couldn't say nothing about it, couldn't fight back against it. The house woulda fall down if he did. I already knew he wasn't home. He never stay in the house when his father was like that—which probably make his father's blood boil even more. He was either in the car yard or at Mitt's parlour at the end of Manger Street.

The parlour was closer, so I made my way there. Mitt was hardly ever there those days. He had two sons to pick up the slack for him. One was sweeping up the front with a cocoyea broom. The other was manning the counter. Tiki was there, two little boys next to him. They was all huddled around the *Street Fighter II* machine. Tiki was playing against the computer. The boys was cheering him on. Sometimes parents would send their children to buy bread and cigarettes and the money would be long lost in that arcade cabinet. People even blow out all their maxi-taxi money over that game. I stood there watching for a while, but Tiki ain't even acknowledge me.

I wasn't sure if he was upset more because of what happen the night before or because his father was ransacking the whole house. I was just shuffling my feet behind him, hoping he would say something. I know Tiki ain't the type to hold no grudges. He also don't like nobody apologizing to him, so it's hard to talk to him when he's angry with you.

"Gimme a coin," I tell the boy at the counter. I put a dollar down.

The boy at the counter hesitated. "This is your money or Sam money?"

All that bread and cigarette money—I probably wasted so much of it on these machines. Sam gave Mitt's sons a good shake-up one day, told them to ban me from playing the arcades. I nudged the bill forward, "All mine."

He took the dollar, slide a token over to me. "Feel you could really beat him?"

"He can't even beat an egg."

The other boys laughed, calling out to Tiki, "You lettin she call you out so?"

As I put the token in the machine, Tiki looked at me cut-eye. I stood shoulder to shoulder with him. He picked Chun Li. "You feel you gonna beat me with that tai chi pigtail-bun bimbo?" I asked him.

He snort out a chuckle. He had to bite his lip to hold it back. I picked Ryu. He muttered, "At least I ain't no lame Karate Kid wax-on-wax-off wannabe."

The match started. Tiki was playing hard, mashing buttons like a madman. The boys was shouting, *Do a Hadouken! Do a spinning kick!* The adrenalin get the best of me and I nearly damn ring the whole joystick out the machine. The whole cabinet was shaking. But no matter how hard Tiki tried, he wasn't gonna win. I simply had more practice. Tiki was too much of a good boy to spend the bread money to play games.

I wasn't even watching the screen when I landed the K.O. on him, thirty seconds still left on the clock.

"Shit," he muttered out, giving the buttons one last flurry of mashes as if that was gonna do something. He stood akimbo, watching his bruised, battered fighter fly up and hit the ground in slo-mo. He shook his head, giving me a small smile.

The boy at the counter shouted out, "You let a girl beat you! Lame!"

"Rematch!" the other boys was cheering.

I was half-expecting Tiki to say shit like he let me win though I knew he was always above that. He turned his pockets inside-out. "Poverty, fellas," he said.

"Want to take a walk?" I asked him.

"Not by no chicken farm this time, right?"

I let out a laugh. "I'm done with that."

"Thank God." He peer up at the sky. "Her brain has returned."

We went down to the end of the road, where this small pond was. You could hear the chanting from the mosque in the distance. This used to be a sacred place till people started dumping off their old fridges and TVs there. One person began doing it and then everybody follow suit. Tiki picked up a twig and slashed it across the water, making a koi fish skitter to the top.

I clear the moss off a rock so I could sit. I tell him everything— had to make sure he get the story cool and clear from me. You never know how people could twist things.

"So when you suppose to start this pig farm thing?" he said, dipping the twig near some guabines.

I skip a stone across the pond. "Tomorrow. After school."

He clicked his tongue. "Pressure."

"I telling you—Sam gone mad."

"You look for it," he said. "Tell you not to bother with them fowls."

I skip another stone. "Didn't even find nothing there."

He looked at me. "At least you try. You could say that. You probably do more than the police."

I shrugged, my gaze falling on a broken Panasonic screen. I saw my dull reflection in it. I remembered the stacks of paperwork back at the station. They solve so much things on the TV. Every episode they find a killer. They have to. If they ain't find no killer, what's the point of watching the show? I wasn't sure if Dumpling's killer woulda ever turn up. I had to be smart. I couldn't be dragging Tiki into this chaos anymore. I hoped the worst had already pass for him—because I know the worst for me was still to come. Worse than the farm. Worse, because at least the farm was only one week. I had to put up with Alma Reese at school. Just thinking about it, I felt drained.

Tiki got up and sat next to me. "The farm have a name?"

"Yeah. Sty Trail Farm."

He skip another stone on the water. "They sell ham round Christmas, right?"

"So I hear."

"Lemme ride down with you tomorrow. That might ease the pain a lil. What you say?"

I nodded, giving him a smile. He then gave me a big cheer-up wink. I felt bad that Tiki was the one who had to ease up things for me. I knew that when he had to go home, he had to pick up pieces of plates and ceramic and glass. But I coulda never get him to talk about any of it. Not straight out. He mighta make a joke like, *Time to clear out the warzone,* but that was it.

"You going home now?" I knew he wasn't, but I still asked.

"I don't think Hurricane Kangal over yet."

"You could help me do something then."

"What's that?"

I tell him, "Let's go get my damn bike back."

"This better not be no trick to get me back to that farm."

"Nah. Told you, I'm done."

CHAPTER 12

IS LIKE EVERYBODY GONE A LIL CRAZY AT THE SAME TIME.

I waited for near half hour but Tiki never show up at the water tower the next morning. I already knew—the rest of the day was going to be hell. I don't know if I was mad at him or not. Wasn't like he promise or anything like that. But really, it wasn't like Tiki to go against his word. When Tiki say he was going to do something, you coulda bet your bottom dollar on it. The boy was loyal. Even to his father, he was loyal. He was one of those people—the type where you know God was having a good day when He make them. The days Tiki didn't come to school, was only because Mr. Kangal fall down in a ditch somewhere.

I rode to school by myself. When we had gone to retrieve the bike from the bushes, I was surprised to see it in one piece. I was at least expecting the Joker card to be lost. But there it was—Sam's message spinning with the wind: *Keep your balance, keep moving!*

When I got to school, I just stood there looking up at the building. Never before I felt so small standing before it—it was like a mouth of steel and concrete—students filtering through. I feel like I coulda hear everybody talking at the same time. Voices building, my head pounding. I couldn't do it, couldn't make it. I didn't want to face everybody. I was sure they all knew about what happened.

It ain't take long to decide what I was going to do. I looked around to see if anybody was watching. Then I picked a direction and rode off. I wasn't one to skip school just like that, but it wasn't worth it. Not that day. Nobody was going to miss me anyway. I didn't know where I was going. Had nowhere to go. Couldn't go home. I didn't even want to imagine what would happen if Sam catch me.

I knew where Tiki woulda be—well, I had a good idea. If he wasn't in school, he was at his uncle's car yard. Tiki couldn't bear to be doing nothing. That was the kinda person he was. So, I rode down there, took only ten minutes.

The yard was a wide open area where the soil was cracked

and the grass was brown. The breeze was always blowing. Only the concrete part of the yard was shaded. There was something about being there that I knew Tiki liked. The air carried sound there. You coulda hear the trees. As soon as I walked into the compound, Raja had his eyes on me. "You cuttin school now?" he asked me. At his feet was a cage with a big, leaf-green iguana. He saw me watching it. "You like him? I name him Draco. Say hello to the nice chicken thief, Draco."

I narrow my eyes at him but didn't say nothing back. I asked him, "Tiki here?"

He let out a scoff. "I don't want Tiki associating with no chicken thief. He too good for you."

"And I don't want my brother associating with no asshole," I tell him. "So that make us even."

He laughed, his tongue hanging out as if this was what he was hungry for—confrontation. Well, I wasn't going to let him have it. I was lucky because Tiki come into view at the same time. He was at the back, his head buried beneath a bonnet. He nearly hit his head as he raised it up. His cheeks and hands was slicked with oil.

"Cool it," he said as he walk up. I wasn't sure if he was talking to me or Raja. He said to me, "You lose your balls? You can't go to school without me?"

"I ain't want to deal with nobody in school today."

With no apology in his voice, he tell me, "So you ain't have no problem terrorizing a madman, his son and his dog, but you shitting yourself over somebody talkin shit to you in school."

I bowed my head. "I wasn't terrorizing nobody. Don't say that."

He nodded, slumping his back as if a sudden wave of regret was weighing him down. I didn't take none of it to heart. I know it was just the anger talking. He led me away from the yard and from Raja. We went to a spot where there was a long stretch of land overgrown with weeds and with slagheaps of rusted iron and corpses of trucks. He stopped at this old Toyota Corolla. The front looked like someone blow up a bomb under the hood but the rest of the car was tip-top. He took a metal rod from a pile of scraps, which looked like it was once a coat hanger. He began to waggle open the driver's side with it. As he was doing so, he said, "For all you know, nobody in school know a thing."

"Tiki, I know people know. News travel faster than a dog scrambling to lick its own ass in that place."

He finally got the door open. He went inside. I hesitated. He looked right at me and said, "The car ain't going to blow up." So he sat in the driver's seat, me in the passenger side. He fiddle around with some wires and actually got the car to start. I was impressed—amazed even. The thing looked like it didn't even have an engine. He turned the radio on to this Jon Secada tune and we push our seats back.

"When last you talk to Nick?" he asked me.

"He barely been home. Why?"

"Apparently he and Raja hatching some kinda plan to mess up Rita."

My mind went back to Flambeau. Rita dancing at the bar, pouring beer into Salaman's mouth. "You sure they wasn't talking shit?"

"I overhear them scheming up something. Raja want Nick to go down to Sundew and play like he going as a client. Raja pay him a hundred dollars."

"A hundred dollars to do what?"

He shrugged again. "Ask your brother. And tell him to be careful unless he want his head cut off."

"You think that's a true story?"

"What? That Salaman cut a man head off?"

"Yeah."

"We ain't gonna know till we find Nick's head floating in the river."

"Nick need to cool it," I said. "Raja too."

Tiki was quiet for a while, contemplative. He then said, "You know, sometimes I look round at everybody and wonder how they come out so."

"I know what you mean," I said, my hand resting on his shoulder.

He scratch the back of his head. "Is like everybody gone a lil crazy at the same time. And because it happen at the same time, nobody really notice."

"At least one person notice, Tiki."

"I have to. Or I going to turn out just like them. I have to be the sane one." I thought about Nick for a moment. And how Sam had said that at least one of us had to turn out all right. I had to be that one. "I ain't even allow to get angry in my house. Only my father alone allowed to do that. If I get vex once around him, he gonna just throw it back in my face. Like I am the crazy one."

Tiki turned away from me. But I knew he was tearing up a little. He was quiet for a few seconds but then continued, "He was studyin to be a doctor once—my father. Once upon a time, when he was young. Wanted to help people. But look at him now—he just a piece of shit now." He put his hair over his forehead. "I look at men in Kukuyo, all over Trinidad and see the same thing. Like it have this shadow, this beast snatching them up and killin them off in a way."

I shift my body closer to his. I move to put my arm around him but changed my mind once I saw his shoulder tense up. I just kept rubbing his back. "You worry you'll turn out that way?" I asked him. "Because you ain't like that. Not at all. And never will be. I know that in my heart."

He didn't say anything. I wasn't sure if I was saying the right thing. This used to happen—the truth peeking out through the fractures. You couldn't get Tiki to be serious about anything with his father most of the time. You had to wait till moments like these to get a glimpse—before the cuts seal back up. You couldn't prod at the wound.

My mind flipped back to Nick, when Moonesar had expel him. Up till then, I wasn't really worried for Nick. I hated when he and Sam had words with each other but I didn't think it was a real problem back then. "I think someone snatch up Nick a long time ago. He still in there somewhere. This beast, it couldn't take all of him," I said to Tiki. He bowed his head. I asked, "You know how Nick got kick outta school?"

He nodded. "Ms. Petra. The boys used to say she had a legendary bottom."

"And Nick wanted to be an even bigger legend when he lift up her skirt for the class to see. That's when Ms. Petra left."

"Yeah. I remember."

I let out a scoff. I didn't like to imagine how it all went down. "I remember Sam had asked him that same day he got expel, You want to be known as this person? Well, to me, it better to be nobody than to be the person who get kick out of school for exposing the teacher's panties. Nick was poison after that, you know. Legend, my ass. Nobody wanted to talk to him after that. Well, nobody except one person."

Tiki sighed. "Raja."

I nodded. "Since that day I knew I had to be sane one. I feel what you feel, like everything just get crazy. Maybe it was always this way and we just getting old enough to see it. This thing with Dumpling—that get so crazy too. I swear, the whole thing made so much sense in my head at the time. I wasn't being smart. Play stupid games, win stupid prizes. Now I have to shovel pig shit as my prize."

I got a laugh out of him for that. "You think you gonna be all right?"

I shrugged then gave him a nod. "Sam's just looking out for me."

"It's nice to have someone look out for you." He scratched his head. "So you ain't upset with him no more?"

"Hell yeah, I'm still mad."

"Still want me to go with you?"

I looked at him, then brushed his hair from his eyes. "I'll be all right. You have your own things to do. I think the worst of it's already gone."

CHAPTER 13

YOU READY TO GET DIRTY, WOLFGIRL?

S ty Trail Farm was just off the main road, kind of in the middle of nothing. Just a long stretch of bush and fence and light poles. I dragged myself and my bike up the trail. The path was lined with short woven wire fences, a half dozen cows grazing inside, chewing their cuds. The path wasn't long, not even half as long as the one that led to the poultry farm. The smell was twice as bad though. I stood there for a minute, watching the cows from the distance. They was so calm—watching them eased my mind.

As I approach the stead, I saw Baram sitting on the porch, bolstered up on a rocking chair. It's a wonder of the world, that chair—how it manage to hold all that weight. Swear, I ain't never see anybody fat like Baram before. With a heavy snort, he propped himself up and let out a loud, gravelly laugh. "The big, bad wolf sheself, boy!"

The house rested along an incline, in such a way that the front half was touching the ground and the back had to be supported by stone pillars. Behind the house was a tall, yellow palisade and behind the palisade, was a series of sheds where the hogs was milling around. You coulda hear the uuck-uuck from where I stood.

Baram motion for me to come inside. "I hope you pack good clothes in that bag."

My bag was already filled to the brim with textbooks thick like the tomes of Vedas. Nevermind I didn't use any of them that day. I felt so stupid that bringing clothes ain't even cross my mind.

I didn't realize I was dying of thirst till I spot the metal jug of ice water sitting on the porch. Baram poured me a glass, and I downed it in one gulp before I follow him out to the palisade. The gate was already wide open. The smell from the sheds was so bad that my nose felt like it coulda crawl up into my skull. Baram patted my back, saying, "You ready to get dirty, wolfgirl?"

I gave him a hard look. A red flag went up in my head. Didn't sound right, how he say that. I knew I had to watch my back.

The yard was fenced off. The grunting was non-stop—*uuck, uuck, uuck*. Farther in was a grid of sixteen empty pens shaded by a wide iron roof. Baram point to the squashed, soiled hay lining each pen. "Lesson one," he said. "Pigs like to sleep in hay. Clean hay. So this hay? It need to go. No time to waste."

I just looked at him, putting my hair in a ponytail. "What you want me to do?"

"Pick it up—what else?"

I looked at him cross-eye. "With what?"

"Your hands, what you feel?"

I twist my mouth. He laugh and pointed to the pitchfork lying in the corner. Next to it was a large bale of hay. I stared at it for a while, like I had gone catatonic. "Come, wolfgirl!" Baram clapped his hands. "We hafta move!"

I unhooked my school skirt and unbutton my blouse. Just in a white cotton undervest and short pants now, I packed my uniform into my bag.

"That is what you wearin?" Baram asked.

I continued zipping up my bag, not bothering to reply. I grabbed the pitchfork and went to work. Wasn't long till my legs was splattered with mud. Baram pulled up a stool, his eyes on me like glue. "Excuse me if I outta place but I just hafta say somethin."

"What?"

"How old you is?"

I hesitate. "Fifteen."

"Fifteen and ain't wearin a bra. That ain't right."

I wipe my brow, taken aback. "What you mean?"

"What you mean, what I mean? Everything printin out. How you have youself right now, it ain't right."

"Speak for yourself. Your breasts way bigger than mine. You ain't hearing me telling you to get a bra." I know I shoulda be shutting my mouth but he look like he coulda take it.

His eyebrows shot straight up as he let out a loud Santa Claus chuckle. "You could gimme all the talks in the world. That don't change what seen as proper."

"Me shovelling pig shit ain't proper."

I wasn't wearing no bra, partly because I never had nobody to buy them for me. Sam was no good. The first time I get my period, he was more freak out than me. This coming from the man who raise my mother. The ones Sam used to buy was never comfortable. And I was never comfortable with him buying them anyway—but I didn't really know nobody else to ask. He gave me money once to do it myself and I couldn't do it. I think his discomfort rubbed off on me. I learn to see it as a blessing, almost. I know it's a thing that girls want to be into but the whole thing look like too much stress for me.

"Bible say pigs is filthy creatures," Baram was telling me as I untied the bale and spread the hay. "Look, I am Hindu and I ain't mean to badtalk the Bible. But the people in the Bible ain't know what them talkin bout half the blasted time. If Leviticus and them other fellas did mind pig, they woulda know that pig just don't feel right tramplin bout in their own mess. You know what does eat its own caca? Rabbits. But I ain't seeing the Bible beatin down the Easter Bunny."

He helped me with the other pens, having me clean while he spread the new hay himself. I had to endure a steady succession of stale jokes while we worked. The kind that was so bad you had to laugh. But I didn't want him to catch a grin outta me. He laugh at all his own jokes, however.

What you call a sleeping bull? A bull-dozer.

What happen to the frog car after he park it? It get toad.

The sun was already setting by the time we finish. He led me to the yard behind the sheds. When I went in, a bunch of the pigs scamper up to me, rubbing their snouts against my knees, looking up to me with small watermelon-seed eyes. Baram clapped his hands and they took his lead, arranging themselves into a queue before marching back to their pens and nestling on the hay. I ain't gonna lie, it was a sight.

When he was done, he said, "Careful you get the ringworm. You need to go and wash youself off."

He motion for me to follow him to the back of the house where two large ribbed water tanks sat on stone pedestals. A series of PVC pipes connected both. He turned a faucet attached to one and water began to gush down from the tank, splashing onto the concrete. A broken slab of blue soap rested on a small paint bucket near the water. There was no galvanize cubicle here. No plastic curtain. No privacy.

Baram had his eyes set on me. I knew the look. "Wolfgirl, what you waitin for?" he asked.

Time slow down for that moment and I felt like I coulda see each individual drop hit the ground, each one letting out its own thunder. I looked him right in the eye. "You ain't serious, right? You gonna stand right there?"

"Hurry up and clean youself. You wastin mi water!" I turned my gaze to the muddy splotches on his trousers, the tiny strands of hay sticking out of his shoes.

"I not gonna do that while you gaping at me," I tell him straight, clutching my vest.

"Gaping at what? You gettin me vex now!"

"Mister, if you come one step closer, I will kick you in the balls."

He shook his head. "What that hafta do wit washin youself off? Look, move so." He pushed me out of the way and washed his hands and feet.

I let out, "You mean, wash my feet—" and stopped myself, a

great wave of shame overcoming me. I gave him an apologetic smile.

"What you thought I mean?" he asked. "You want a proper shower? I have one inside the house, but water fraid to come outta it today. You can't be bathin outside here for any old body to see. You mad or what? Your mother ain't teach you that?"

While washing my feet, I replied, "I only have my grampa."

"So what happen—your mother dead?"

I hesitated. "Yeah."

"Sorry to hear that but somebody round here shoulda teach you that."

He fiddled inside his pocket and pulled out twenty dollars. "First day on the job, you do good," he said, handing it to me. "Save it, spend it, I ain't care. But no need to tell gramps. We better get goin before it start to get dark." I wasn't expecting to get anything from the man, but really, twenty dollars wasn't near enough for this shit.

I followed him to a shed at the back of his house, changed back into my school uniform and stashed the dirty clothes into a plastic bag. He tied a double-knot on it and tossed it into his pickup. He then help get my bike into the tray.

The drive back to my house was quiet. Baram didn't play the radio and the only times I spoke was to give him directions. The engine was sputtering so much that I swear the whole vehicle woulda fall apart before we even reach halfway back. It was a miracle it got there in one piece. When he pulled up to the house, Zandolee was already making his rounds. He stopped his pacing as he eyed the pickup, crinkling his nose as the headlights shone directly on him. Baram muttered out, "This young boy dunno he could get bounce down like that?"

I thanked him and hopped out, ran right inside without looking back. It felt so good to be home. I was so tired I just wanted to flop down on my bed. Inside, the TV was blaring *The Bold and the Beautiful*. Sam was in his recliner. "How it was?" he asked.

"Four days left," I said, hurrying right past him and into my room.

CHAPTER 14

THE GIRL IS STILL HUMAN. BUT I AIN'T SURE ABOUT YOU NO MORE.

L ater that night, I came out my room to see Nick sitting on the floor, his back slumped against the recliner, where Raja sat. I'd heard them come in but Raja wasn't the kinda person I'd come out to say goodnight to. He had a bottle of fried channa in his hand. He reached down, shaking some into Nick's palm. *Knight Rider* was on but neither of them was watching. As I made my way to the kitchen, they turned to me but they ain't say nothing. I was a little surprised—I at least expected Raja to say some smart shit. Their conversation was too important to bother with me. I poured some corn flakes, sat at the table and pretended like I was watching the TV.

"Pan see you?" Raja asked Nick.

Nick took a while to respond. "I dunno. I wasn't lookin." The words dribbled out of his mouth. Like after each couple of words he wanted to retch.

"He probably thought you couldn't get it up. What you think?"

"I dunno. But I don't think he see—"

"You might as well kill yourself if you can't get it up. That's like the beginning of the end. What you think, Nick? You would kill yourself if that happen?"

Nick's expression didn't change. He just kept his eyes on the TV. It cut to a commercial—a PSA about payphone vandalism, a reggae song blaring, *Wicked! Wicked!*

Raja said, his mouth full of channa, "You know the bitch does do it just to make me look like an ass. She willing to sleep with a mule if it mean to tarnish my name."

Nick shook his head. "She just doing it to feed herself, man."

Raja nudged him with his foot. "You gettin smart with me?"

"Naw. I just think we mighta gone too far back there."

"Yo, you could imagine how much people laughin at me when they see she? And knowin—once upon a time—I was gonna marry that?"

"She ain't tell them to laugh at you. Is not her fault."

"Then who fault it is?"

"Nobody." Nick got up.

Raja held his palm up. "Sit back down. We having a conversation."

"Nothin left to talk bout." Nick was without pause now. "I gonna tune out."

Raja got up, his car keys jingling as he got them out. He play-punched Nick in the shoulder, saying, "Listen. Nick, you was a true friend tonight. Don't fret bout the girl. You dunno she like how I know she. She always had issues. She grandfather rape she when she was—"

Nick's gaze fell upon me. He cut Raja off, "Okay, okay."

Raja noticed me as well. "Yeah, okay," he said and he was out the door. Nick went in his room.

As I sat there, finishing the corn flakes, there was a knock on the door. I wasn't feeling to answer it, thinking it was just Raja returning for something he had forgot. But then the knocking turned into rattling, like a train was rolling by. I set my bowl down and opened the door.

It was Rita.

Eyes glowing and blood-flecked, face soft and soggy like a bruised fig. Looking like a bus knock her down. She was breathing hard like she was about to burst through her top and transform into the Incredible Hulk. When I saw her, I swear all the blood flow outta me. I turned pale like iced kingfish, I was so scared.

My gut reaction was to shut the door but she barge right into the house like a rhino.

"Nick!" I called out. Couldn't do nothing else.

Nick came bumbling out from the back. As soon as Rita cast her eyes on him, it was like she was seeing red. She lunge right at him, grating her knuckles against his collarbone. I jump back as the scuffle dragged into the kitchen. They knocked the corn flakes bowl right to the floor in the fracas. Nick had his elbows crossed over his face the whole time, yelling out, "Stop! Stop!"

She dug her nails into his wrists. The long blue veins on her palms throbbing as she started to hammer away at his jaw, loud gurgling noises spilling out from her throat. He was like a backyard fowl scrambling away from a hatchet. He couldn't get her off— couldn't overpower her. She was small compared to him, but anger like what she had coulda grant superpowers. The girl was out to tear him apart, rip out his entrails, leave him on the carpet like roadkill.

Nick finally managed to break loose and ran to the door but she catch him again. She had him in a headlock. They rolled onto the porch outside. I ran after them.

It was only then I saw the other figure standing in the street. The shoes, rat-chewed, caked with mud, laces missing. It was Salaman, both his hands in his pocket. I could almost hear the coins in there clinking, clinking.

Rita shoved her palm against Nick's nose, bending the ball of it so much that I swear it was gonna snap right off. He sink his teeth into her hand before it could.

She screamed out and Nick flipped her over, jamming his thumbs against her neck.

At the same time, Sam came dashing out of his room, his paunch jutting out through his open shirt. "Cut the shit!" he bellowed as he lifted Nick and hauled him to the side.

As soon as Nick was down, Rita charged at him again. There wasn't no stopping her.

Sam vaulted in, wrapping his arms around her chest, grappling with her as she kicked the air, kicked her shoes off, cussing. Cussing Nick. Cussing me. Cussing Sam. Cussing God. Sam yanked her to the gate, her heels grating against the concrete.

"Go from here!" he said, pushing her into the street. She fell to her side.

Salaman helped her up, putting his arm around her. He gave Sam a small nod before walking away. Sam locked eyes with him till he disappeared around the corner, hobbling with Rita under his shoulder.

At the same time, Nick sat on the porch, thumbing a tag of bloody skin on his left elbow. A large hyphen of purple on his collarbone. He reached into his pocket to get his cigarettes and he lit up right there like nothing had just happen.

Sam was still in the street, making sure they was gone. He was still trying to catch himself. Same with me. Boss Das came up to the fence. "Sammy, everything under control over there?"

Sam folded his arms, trying to conceal his heavy breathing, his heaving chest. "I think so."

"What the bloomin hell happen just now?"

Sam eyed Nick. "We'll find out just now."

"If they come back, call me so I could get ready with the tyre iron," Das said before he went back to his house.

Sam's eyes cut right into Nick again. "Boy, if you don't start talkin—"

"Is nothing," Nick said, taking a puff.

"A madwoman come storming into my house ready to strangle you to death, and that is nothing to you?" Sam pinched the cigarette out of Nick's mouth. I almost expected him to crush it in his fist, how mad he looked, up till the second he flicked it away. Sam pointed to me. "See that girl there? That is your little sister. This is the example you settin for she?"

Nick let out a sigh, his shoulders slumping. Not that kinda annoyed *Oh God, don't talk to me* sigh. Just this sound of defeat. I went up to him and put my hand on his shoulder. I usually didn't want to get between Sam and Nick. For my own sake, mostly. I couldn't stand it when they was like this. Sam was ready to blow right the hell up. I dunno if Nick was drunk or not but he needed to start talking. He pulled out another cigarette and looked at Sam as if asking permission with his eyes. Sam hesitated but eventually gave him the nod and Nick lit up. He took a big pull. "It was Raja's idea," he said, blowing out the smoke.

No shit, I wanted to say. Sam nodded so I believe he was thinking the same thing—but that wasn't helping Nick. "If Raja tie a rope round his prick and jump from a bridge, your jackass self going to do it too?" Sam said.

"Sam, let him tell the story," I said. And he was quiet after that.

"I went to Sundew and rent a room," Nick began.

"Why you went there?" I cut in.

He pursed his lips, eyeing me hard. "Rune, just let me tell the frigging story."

"Sorry."

"I went to see Rita, the girl Raja used to be with."

"She working there now?" Sam asked.

"Yes. A little while now. And before you say anything else— no, I didn't go to shack up with nobody." Nick started rubbing his face. "It was just suppose to be a joke. I dunno."

I wanted to bring up Lambi but I kept my trap shut. It seem Nick had learn nothing from that day. He continued the story, "She was different. I ain't talk to the girl in so long—feel like dog years. In the back of my mind, I was wonderin if she realize nothing good was gonna come of this—is not like she ain't know I was Raja's friend— his drinking partner ... So ... I put the money under the ashtray."

"Money from where? Money to do what?" Sam cut in.

I said, "Let him tell the story, Sam."

"Raja give me two hundred dollars. I put it under the ashtray and Rita went in the bathroom. Tidying up. I tell the girl that I had a special request, that I want her to go in the wardrobe. And to come out and surprise me. She asked me if it was some kinda trick and I throw in an extra hundred." He took another drag. "I was kinda shock she take the money. Then she get up from the bed and went over to the wardrobe. She turned to me and asked how long she have to be in there for me to feel surprised. Well, I asked her what kinda question is that. You do what you do. Is a surprise, I tell her. So she start to hesitate, saying how the wardrobe was too dark. But she still went in. Then I close the door."

My stomach started to hurt as he said that. I know I wasn't going to have nobody lock me in no dark closet. You could give me a million dollars—no way I'm doing that. I couldn't imagine how hard up for money she had to be for her to do that.

Nick continued, "She wasn't in there alone. Raja had this ..." He hesitated, swallowing hard, like the words was cutting his throat. He took another drag, then the words blew out with the smoke, "Raja had this iguana. So I put it in there. And the girl went crazy."

"Nick." I coulda just say his name because I didn't have the words.

"You leave the girl in there?" Sam didn't even sound angry anymore. Just sombre.

"I panic," Nick said, bowing his head. Nick was tearing up, I could see it even though he started rubbing his face again to mask it. "She was cussing loud-loud for the whole building to hear, sounding like somebody was killin she. I panic and just run right out."

I didn't know the girl, and didn't even like the little I know about her, but I feel it for Rita—I really did. Still do. I pictured her in there, the skin of her bottom brushing against the dust. Balling her palms into fists, heart beating fast. She wasn't in there alone, Nick say. I could imagine the moment she feel it—the tail brushing past her toes and how she probably slam her hips against the door, swaying like a cracked bell. Confused as a fart in a hurricane.

When Nick finish the story, Sam didn't say anything. He looked up at the moon, stayed like that for a minute or two. When he was done, he looked Nick right in the eye and said, "I was going to call the police for her. But if they come and hear this story, they would quicker lock you up than she."

Nick hung his head low like a sorry dog.

Sam began shaking his head and didn't stop. "That ... whatever it was you do back there—that ain't normal, is all I have to say. It don't matter what line of work the girl is in. The girl is still human. But I ain't sure about you no more. I shame for you."

I ain't say it. But I was too.

CHAPTER 15
MAKE A HOLE.

Tiki didn't come to school the next day either. But I wasn't gonna miss two days in a row. I told myself to stop being a coward. Alma Reese and Krissy Kanhai come up to me as soon as I put my bag down on my desk. They stood there, talking to each other, pretending I wasn't there. "You mind chickens, girl?" Krissy asked Alma.

"I have a few in the yard," Alma said. "But when I wake up this mornin, they was gone!"

"They disappear? Where you think they went?"

"Well, I hear it have something lurkin in the bush."

"Hmm, some kinda rodent?"

"Sound so. Thought it was a rat at first. But when I see it, it wasn't no rat."

Krissy raise her eyebrows. "What it was?"

Alma flash a quick glance at me, her mouth curling like a snake. She point at me and shouted out, "An ugly, black mongoose!"

Alma nearly fall over at her own outburst. Some others in the room laugh too but I don't think they even know what they was laughing at. "Look like you have a new name!" Krissy said to me. "What sound a mongoose does make?"

"*Kiiiiiiiiiii!*" Alma screech.

My blood was boiling but I ain't say nothing. But saying nothing could backfire easy.

In class, Alma and Krissy sat a few tables behind me. I had the zen-like patience of the goddess Sita for most of the day. But last period, Maths class, I reach my limit. Alma was still making that grating hissing sound—*kii kiiii kii*. I tense up my shoulders, biting my tongue. It was only Alma doing this crap by then. It get old for Krissy after an hour. Everybody else was busy going about the rest of their life, taking notes from the board.

Alma louder this time—*Kiiiiiiiii!*

The teacher, Ms. Parasram, ain't lift an eyebrow. Teachers

never notice crap like this—only if you passing notes or chewing gum. *I am an educator, not an exorcist.* That was Parasram's favourite line. It didn't make sense to tell her nothing. I turned around to give Alma a scowl, my war face.

Alma flash me the middle finger and mouth to some boys next to her, "The mongoose gettin rabid."

I put my head down, counting down the minutes for the last bell. When school was finally over, all the children ran out to the maxis in the main road. I hated that the day wasn't really over for me. Out of the frying pan and into the trough of pig shit. I leaned against the flagpole, glaring at everybody. Boys swinging their bookbags at each other, girls tiptoeing along the edge of the sidewalk. I didn't want to talk to nobody. I didn't want to see nobody.

I got to my bike and sped off.

Baram was waiting for me as usual. He rose up from his rocking chair and come up to greet me. I dodge him, jostling past the side of his house to the palisade at the back. Didn't even make eye contact. I flung my bag on a concrete slab. My face was hot, minted with sweat. I was struggling so bad to take off my school blouse that I nearly pop the buttons right off.

Baram approach me. "Why yuh mouth swell up like a jep fly inside and sting it?"

I didn't say nothing—if I did, I feel I woulda let out a hard cuss. I continued to fumble with the buttons.

He had a big frown now. "I could trust you to feed me pigs today? Because I feel like you go poison them!"

I finally jerked the buttons loose and crumpled my blouse and shoved it into my bag. I had a T-shirt underneath this time. I let out a growl, "Why this place have to smell like shit all the time?"

"It smellin like shit cause is shit we hafta clean up. That there is the objective."

He went into the house, beckoning for me to follow him. He

gave me a glass of cold water and gesture for me to sit at the kitchen table. The kitchen wasn't so much a kitchen as it was a stove and sink lying across an alcove covered with soot and spiderwebs. A tall stack of old newspapers was stuffed into a corner. Nailed flat against the wall was a crumpled pair of child pyjama pants. It was dark blue and had yellow stars and moons on it. I couldn't take my eyes off of it. Was hung up almost as if it was a painting.

I took a sip of the water, trying to calm myself down.

"You gonna tell me what the matter is?"

I took a longer sip. I brushed off the question, asking, "What work we hafta do today?"

He shook his head. "I ain't think you in any type of workin condition, lil lady."

I began tapping a beat on the kitchen table, my eyes still on the pyjamas. We was quiet for a while. But the silence was worse than anything. He noticed me watching the pants again. "The pants belong to my niece," he began.

I crinkled my brow. "Why they on the wall?"

"My niece dead many years ago. She was wearing the pants when she die." He rubbed his face.

I didn't want to hear about a dead little girl, but I couldn't say so. It was awkward. He began telling me regardless, "My sister and her husband get themself in a bad smash-up on the highway. Was the other person who was drunk. He survive, they die on the spot. I wasn't so close with either of them but she still wanted me to be godfather to the niece."

"What was her name?"

"Rebecca. She was five." He swallow hard. "So was up to me to take care of the child. It ain't have much here but I try my best, could tell you that. One day she wake me up and tell me she was gettin trouble breathing. I went to see if I coulda call the doctor. Next thing I see was she lyin on the ground. I woulda take her to the hospital right then and there but my vehicle was outta commission and I was scraping everywhere for money at that time. Couldn't even buy proper clothes for the child. So I call the doctor and he tell me she probably get sting or eat something she was allergic to. The doctor say that her throat was probably closing up and the most important thing to do was to keep the girl calm and part of that was for me to stay calm. How a man could stay calm when a little girl turnin pale right before he eyes?"

He shifted in his chair, his eyes on the pyjama pants the whole time now. He continued, "After a few minutes, she wasn't breathin at all. Time was runnin out. He said he would call an ambulance but that I had to do something in the meantime. He ask me if I was good with my hands, so I tell him yeah. He ask me if I fraid blood, so I tell him it depend on who blood he talkin bout. He tell me to get a razorblade—a small, clean one—and a straw. He was tellin me how I could make a hole in her throat and breathe into it through the straw. He use them words too, I remember. *Make a hole.*" He paused, then looked at me, letting out a nervous chuckle. "And I was just like—this madman want me to cut this little girl's throat. Right then and there. I went to get to the blade but I didn't have the belly to do it. She die right there on the floor."

"I'm sorry." I was breathing hard.

He let out another nervous chuckle, looking up at the pants again. "I sorry too. She probably coulda be alive now if I had money. The pickup woulda be working and she woulda get to the hospital and maybe she'd be here now. But in the end—is all just a whole bunch of woulda, coulda, shoulda. You need money if you want to live in this world. A man without money is no good to nobody. I don't keep the pants there to remember the girl. I keep it to remember my mistake. I want to make sure I never end up in a situation like that ever again. I keep reminders for my mistakes all over." He was smiling but his eyes was telling a different story. "This house just littered with regrets all over. Anything old and broken you might see. People does want to forget, but not me. Everything have a story."

The way he talk, it remind me of that conversation I had with Dumpling. The same unashamed honesty, like he was waiting for a long time to make a connection. I felt strangely better after he told the story. It's odd, realizing how little you know about people. He took my glass to the sink. When he came back, he asked, "So what it is that troublin you?"

After the gravity of his story, I was embarrassed to say. I bowed my head. "Is just children in school."

"Beat you up?"

"No."

"Then what?"

"Just things they saying. I know all of it is just words but—"

"Gimme a name."

"What?"

"Gimme a name. I gonna deal with them."

I scrunch my brow at him. *What the hell he could do?* I was thinking. But I called the name regardless. "Alma."

"What's that?" Baram spit out. "Who gone and name they child Almond?"

I couldn't help it. I bust out laughing. "Al-ma," I said again slowly.

"What the hell this Al-ma sayin?"

"She start this stupid talk, saying I smelly, calling me Mongoose."

He wiped his forehead. "This Alma feel she bad? Let this Alma step into yuh shoes for a minute and we goin to see if she could even pee straight!" I was taken aback because I was expecting him to laugh and tell me to get over it, especially after the story he tell.

He told me to go wash my face. The bathroom looked like it was for duennes, it was so small. Grime and moss on the walls. What catch my attention was the reddish stains under the sink. It was like blood, looked too red to be rust. The water was rattling something down in the drain pipe. When I turned the tap off, I noticed something was stuck down there. But I didn't have time to look.

Baram called me out to the sheds, to a secluded area of the yard. Tethered to a withering mango tree trunk was a giant big-bellied boar. Its snout was the colour of mustard and it looked bigger than even Baram. Our eyes connected. It had this gentleness in its face. But its size still made me anxious. The belly looked like it coulda hold two of me.

"You take a break today," Baram say. "Lemme just get this big one back to the sty."

"He have a name?" I asked.

"Hara."

"Hara? Why Hara?"

"Another name for Shiva. Destroyer of all evil." Baram went over to the boar and untied the rope. As he walk it over to me, I expect it to push its snout toward my knee, but it never did. Baram looked up at the sun. He asked, whittling his voice down, "How much you think big boy here could eat, eh?" He gave the boar's rope a quick tug. "How much pounds?"

Before I could have a chance to answer, he added, "How much pounds of food you think all these pigs could eat in a single day?"

"I can't say."

The boar finally took Baram's lead. I followed behind. "Pigs mightn't be filthy, eh, but they's some greedy beasts. This one here could eat the whole of hell. He does eat anything."

"He eat anything? He eat people too?"

He paused, cringing a little, but then give me a quick smirk.

"Anybody troublin you, you bring they ass here! I could use them as manure." He started to laugh like a hyena. The boar got riled up as well.

Just after he got the boar into the sty, it started to rain heavy. Baram took me inside and shut the doors. He put on the TV and pop a cassette in the Betamax. I was surprised he was still using Betamax because even Sam had upgrade to VHS by this time. Amitabh Bachchan come up on the screen—he was in a suit, in the middle of a field holding a suitcase, three men before him. Some kind of drug deal about to go down.

Baram watched as he prepared a large plate of Crix crackers with sardines for dinner. "Is a classic one here," he said.

At the same time, Big B said, *Aren't you scared of death, Raj Singh?*

As Baram poured two glasses of coconut water, he pointed to the screen. He tell me, "Watch this part!"

At the same time, Big B toss the briefcase at the men and it blow right up, whipping clouds of dust into the air.

"Watchin this home here ain't nothin though," Baram said, laughing. "The real experience is in the cinema house, sittin down in the pit. Next to a woman you like."

There was a moment of silence as the rain beat down on the galvanize above us. I was oddly comfortable in that moment, like I coulda confide in this man. Like every problem I had was ready to melt away. I asked him, "So you not married?"

He answer straight, "A woman could hold a beast like me down?"

"I see worse," I said with a little smile. "It not too late."

Coconut water leak down the side of his mouth as he speak, "I never know much bout gettin a woman and I never know notten bout keepin one. And I ain't goin to trouble meself now with that craziness. I's a bonafide bachelor. Wolfgirl, you's the only lady who come bout in these parts in a real long time."

I gave a small laugh. "The rest of them probably think you gonna feed them to the pigs."

He hesitate to laugh. He ain't say much after that. Right after I was done eating, he switched the movie off and was ready to get me home.

CHÂPTER 16

HUSH. A MAN LIKE ME DO ANYTHING FOR YOU.

The rain was just a cool drizzle by the time Baram got me back home. Not enough to catch a cold from, but enough for the housewives to stay away from their yards and for Zandolee to stay off the corner. As Baram dropped me off he said, "Day off tomorrow. Busy, busy."

I won't lie—I was a little disappointed. I was warming up to the fatso. "What I suppose to do tomorrow then?" I asked him.

"Is your own life to live, wolfgirl," he said. "But tomorrow is a day you ain't needed."

As he drove off, I noticed someone was watching from down the road, hiding behind an old sedan, hugging themselves. I got a closer look and saw that it was Rita.

My feet froze. I couldn't tell if she was hiding or not, but I knew her eyes was right on me. For a moment, I imagined her in that closet again, swinging back and forth against the door like a cracked bell. But she looked calm now, miles from whatever she had morph into the night before. I didn't really blame her for how she reacted. It wasn't the right thing she did, but I didn't blame her.

At first I wanted to wave to her, maybe even approach her. Call it guilt, I dunno. Maybe I coulda apologize for him. I dunno what I wanted. But the rain came down at the same time. Still, she wasn't moving. She was just there, staring. I became a little scared. Even as I was going inside, she didn't budge. I didn't know what to do. So I just called out, "You okay there?"

She jumped in alarm, scampering off as if she didn't know I had notice her.

When I went inside, Sam was in the kitchen. "You hungry?" he asked, getting up with the pan of scrambled eggs.

I shook my head. "Ate already."

He scraped the egg off the pan into a plate of Vienna sausages. "Well, you have to eat again," he said as he set the plate on the table. You couldn't argue with Sam when he cooked. I think it was one of his least favourite things to do. Sam sat opposite me, watching me eat. He asked, "Where the hell you went and eat?"

"Baram make dinner for me."

His eyebrows shot straight up. "So the fat man treatin you good, I see."

"He's all right," I replied, mouth full of sausage.

He nodded. "You understand why I send you there, right?"

I looked at him, giving him a small nod.

He continued, "Too many girls, they put them up to cook and clean. But you ain't no normal girl. That stunt you pull. That was a man stunt. So I wanted to put you to work like a man."

I wished he didn't have to lecture while I was eating. I already wasn't hungry but now I lost my appetite. All I could respond was, "Yes, Sam."

"Nah, I was wrong to be thinkin like that. I don't want you to see work as a punishment. A job is a good thing. Yeah, you have to put bread on the table but the real purpose of a job is to make you fit into the bigger picture. When you do that, you could see everything for the small, good things. You know what I mean, child?"

"I think so."

He steepled his fingers, locked eyes with me. "I make you two a promise the day your mother cremate. I tell you and Nick I'll take care of both of you. I tired sayin this." His voice cracked a little.

"I know."

He lowered his gaze. "Nick is lost. I lose him long time."

"He lose himself," I said.

"He ain't learning. The boy ain't changing."

"He don't believe he have a problem," I tell Sam. "So how he gonna change?"

"He have to hit rock bottom first," Sam said, his gaze trailing to the sink. "I dunno how else he goin to smarten up."

He looked at my half-finished plate. "You done?" he asked. I nodded but he didn't take the plate. "You think you could ask that Kangal boy to see bout Nick gettin into that car yard?"

"If you want me to start asking him for favours, Sam, you have to start calling him by his name. Tiki. That's the boy's name."

I expected him to at least crack a chuckle but he remained serious. "When you see Tiki, ask him bout the car yard. That would be good for Nick."

"If Raja can't get him in, how you expect Tiki to—"

"Raja is a fool," Sam said. "He don't want Nick to do nothin with himself. And Nick is too stupid to see it. People like that is everywhere. They just want to feel better about theyself by keepin everybody else down. I seeing that behaviour my whole life."

I nodded.

Sam finished the meal for me. I helped him with the wares. The rain was done by then. It was dark but wasn't too late. I thought I'd pay Tiki a visit.

As I came out the house, I saw Rita run off again.

I don't even think she saw me—she probably just saw the door open. This time I decided to go after her, see where she was going.

I followed her on foot. I didn't try to hide but I didn't want it to be obvious either. When I cross Gaspar Street, I spotted her in front of Salaman's house, hugging herself as she pushed the gate open with her shoulder. I dunno anyone who's ever been in Salaman's house. I don't think anyone was so brave. Even if a cricket ball landed in the yard, children woulda just pack up and go home. The house was like the dungeon and the Roadster in front of it was the dragon.

The upstairs verandah and furniture was claimed by vines and termites. The chairs was still there, facing each other after so many years. The outdoor staircase was always smudged with black moss. The railing speckled with dried blackbird droppings, probably from birds long dead.

I let a few minutes pass before I went up to the house. The pathway to the front door was feral—grass up to my kneecaps. I tread carefully, on the sharp lookout for snakes and mapepires. My mind racing with each step. Maybe Salaman had bear traps set up in there for all I know. Maybe he had land mines. I could turn back now, I tell myself. I could save myself.

I brushed past the grass and walked around to the back, keeping a lookout for prying neighbours. It have people in Kukuyo who spend nearly their whole life looking out the window, sipping on ginger root tea. I couldn't be sure whether any of them used to ever keep a willing eye on Salaman. The side windows looked as though the frames was about to fall off. It was dark inside. Probably years since that house last seen proper light. The tufted black leather on the upholstery was shredded, warts of sponge leaking out of the furniture.

The backyard was even worse than the front. The walls that enclosed the house was lined with beer bottles, cut and cracked halfway, glimmering like glass teeth. A row of soapstone animal figurines queued up on the final windowsill. It was also the only one with curtains. The louvres was open, a trail of ants marching right through.

I knelt below the sill, slowly raising myself by my toes.

A woman's voice was coming from inside. It was Rita. "It hard to beat," she was saying. "I can't beat it, boy."

I peeped through the mauve organdy curtains. A tye-dye rayon skirt was hanging from the edge of the bed. Two pairs of bare ankles was rubbing against each other. From where I was, I coulda see from the crown of their heads straight down to their feet. Rita was parcelled up in a white coverlet. It wrap around her chest and just above her pelvis, which protrude on both sides, sharp like broken bones.

Salaman was next to her. He ain't bother to cover up. He was playing with the frizzled hairs under his navel. I ain't never see a grown man naked before that. Girls in class was always joking about it. One boy even pull out his thing for the class to see once before he get suspended. But it looked nothing like what I was seeing there, like a dark grey grouper fish cross-stitched onto human skin. It ain't even look like it belong on a wild animal. It looked abnormal, like some kinda growth left untreated for too long. Some scaly fold of skin that was pressed and stretched by a torture device.

Still, I couldn't turn away. I bite down on my tongue. My chest was a furnace. I don't think it was shock. I was afraid to even move. A horsefly was circling my neck and I couldn't even move to bat it away. I admit—a part of me wanted to see everything, no matter how wrong and grotesque the whole situation was. It wasn't because they was naked. I realize that there was more to these two than what I had ingrained in my mind. As repulsed as I was, I see a kind of openness and honesty there I would never have imagined. Maybe that's how Lambi felt with those couples under the bridge. I ain't saying it's right. I'm just saying I found myself in the same boat, and I can't judge now.

Salaman traced his finger along Rita's collarbone and she let out a soft croon—reminded me of a pigeon. She sat up, the blanket falling to her lap, the snake of her backbone facing me. She lit a cigarette and sucked hard on it before blowing the smoke in his face. She made little sucking sounds at him as she slip the cigarette into his mouth and clenched his neck as if to strangle him. She let out a grunt. "Tell me why I here with you? Stink old man. Sometimes I does just lie here and wonder that." Her voice crack at the end.

"Because we have an understanding of each other."

She was lying on her side now, her kneecaps pulled up against his hip. She pinched the cigarette from his lips and took another hard pull. She blow another stream of smoke into his face again.

"I's just meat. You know that? Everybody just eat me up like meat."

"Meat, yeah."

"I goin to hell, you know," she said, taking another drag, "and hell goin to be a room that look just like this one. And plaster up on the walls gonna be pictures of all of this shit."

"You talkin but you ain't thinkin straight," Salaman said, nipping the cigarette from her and crushing the end of it against the side of the bed.

Bzzzzzzz! The fly was in my ear now. I finally swatted at it. Missed.

The same time, Rita grabbed the sides of his neck. "Well, gimme something to think straight."

She got up and put on the stereo. Salaman got up too. They held each other, naked. Soft chutney music started playing. Sundar Popo singing:

Ah scorpion sting me,
ah feelin I go dead
Darlin, if yuh love me,
come lie down in mi bed

They started in a dance, grabbing onto each other as if they was going to both fall down a cliff. She had her arms around his neck, face buried against his chest hair, eyes half-open, staring at his crotch. Smacking her lips. He was playing with her hair, stroking a red welt along her thigh. He clutched a fistful of her hair and whispered something but I couldn't make it out. And it was almost immediate how Rita started to cry.

She was blubbering, "Nobody do anything for me."

"Hush. A man like me do anything for you." Salaman said. He crack a smile, the kind an old man would give a child, and brushed her hair out of her face.

I turned to look over at the neighbours' windows. If somebody was watching and they went back and tell Sam, I was dead. I see enough, I tell myself. I ducked down and slithered out to the front. The rain started to fall again as I crossed into Shepherd Street and ran back to my house.

CHAPTER 17
YOU AIN'T SEE CRAZY YET.

Lunchtime in the grounds the next day the boys was working up a heavy sweat, pelting corkballs at each other. Another crew was ragging up each other near the car park. A couple of girls was twirling around the flagpole, and others on the benches. I sat watching all of it, by myself against the fence, close to the exit gate.

The madhouse was still on my mind. It had me feeling off for the whole day. Tiki was in school that day but we barely talked. When he asked me what was wrong, I told him I had cramps. He gave me a piece of his pawpaw, said it was good for that kinda thing. I couldn't tell him the truth. I felt like I was overbearing enough. So, I had to be alone in my mind with the images of Rita and Salaman splayed out on the bed naked. Fat, old Mr. Moonesar pass me by and I couldn't help but imagine a big, pouting bonito emerging from his crotch.

As I said, I wasn't right in the head at the time. When Alma come up to me, staring me down, snapping her fingers for Krissy to follow, I know I shoulda walk away.

"What you eyeballing me for, Mongoose?" she said.

I bowed my head. "Alma, stop it." It came out in a whisper.

"Stop it? Stop what?"

"Your stupidness."

"What stupidness?"

I looked at her. "Not today."

"Not today?" Krissy said. "What if you dead today? Then when?"

I glared at her. "You might dead today if you don't stop."

Alma and Krissy exchange glances, eyebrows raised.

Alma take a step closer to me, her chin right over my nose. Laughing, she said, "What is that you say, Rat?"

"You hard of hearing?"

She went slack-jawed. "Mongoose gone crazy?" Krissy said,

laughing.

"You ain't see crazy yet," I said.

Krissy step up. "Is threats you throwin, bitch?"

Alma point her finger right against my chest. "Wait till I see you outside school."

"Just leave the girl alone," a voice called out from behind. It was Tiki, knuckles to hips. Superman pose. He had left to get some prunes from the café—for my imaginary cramps. He walk up to Alma. "She telling you to leave her alone, so leave her alone," he said.

Alma replied, "I will beat your ass worse than your father, boy, so watch your mouth."

Tiki's nostrils flare up. He move in like he was about to push her.

I don't know if he really was going to but I jumped in, bookbag in hand. It was automatic.

At the same time, Alma landed a punch—her fist missing me and hitting Tiki's jaw.

There was only a trickle of blood on his lip but still, seeing it make my face go hot. I didn't realize what I do till after I do it.

I swung the bookbag at Alma and it knock the girl straight down to the ground—*braap!*

As I pulled the bookbag back towards me, me and Tiki looked at each other.

Alma on the ground, squirming, skirt up to her belly. She was grumbling something but I wasn't waiting to find out.

Krissy was long gone. Moonesar come racing towards the scene. All in slow motion.

Again, I didn't think—I just ran. Ran like a truck was ready to mow me down. With my bag in hand, I hopped on my bike and bolted right outta the exit gate. Pedalled like I was never coming back.

I rode to Sty Trail Farm. I was drenched with sweat when I

got to the path up to the farm, my legs about to fall off by the time I got there. And just as Baram's house came into view, I stop in my tracks. Had a car parked up at the edge of the track. I recognized it right away.

Cream Buick Regal sedan—Joey's car.

I kept going up the path. The trunk was open but I was too far away to see inside.

Then I remembered—I wasn't suppose to be there that day. Part of me wanted to keep going forward. It was like I was standing before a deep, dark cave. I turned around.

When I got back to the main road, that was when my stomach sank. I wondered why Baram had told me not to come that day. What business he coulda have with Joey Jodha? Wherever Joey went, trouble followed. I didn't want to think of Baram as trouble. Maybe he was in trouble, I thought. My mind was racing with the possibilities. Eventually I thought back to the story—pictured Baram standing over the little girl, the blade in hand, watching her die. The girl in her blue pyjama pants with the stars and the moons. For a moment, I wondered what I woulda done if it was my child. I think I woulda done it. But you can never tell when you actually find yourself in the moment.

If you had ask me the day before if I ever woulda take a swing at Alma, I woulda say no. But as I say, you could never tell till you get to that point.

CHAPTER 18

AT THE CONCLUSION OF IT WAS A BEAST YOU COULDN'T TAKE HOLD OF.

Tiki was waiting for me when I got home. He was sitting on the sidewalk, his back against a lightpole. I froze for a second when I saw him. Before I could say anything, he asked, "Where you had ride off and gone?" He ain't say it accusingly or anything like that, but I still had this pang of guilt in my chest when he say it.

"Moonesar sending we to the gallows?" It took me a while to respond.

"He bring the gallows home to you," Tiki said, pointing his chin behind me. I ain't even notice it—Moonesar's dusty old Ford was parked right behind me. "Thought I'd come and warn you."

I wasn't expecting it to go down so fast. I thought I had at least a day's grace—that Moonesar would call Sam down to the school and it would be handled there. I wasn't expecting the man to actually drive down here.

"Him and Sam inside right now," Tiki said.

"Moonesar know that Alma start the bullshit?"

"Yeah, well, Alma get suspended."

"What about you—"

"Moonesar know how my father could be. He let me off the hook." A small chuckle escape from him. "Is win-win for you. If you don't get suspended, you ain't have to see Alma. If you get suspended, you ain't have to see nobody." I know he was trying to be cheer me up. But I don't think it had anything he coulda say to get me outta the bad mood.

"Tiki, I can't go in there."

"Yes you can. And if you up to it, *Weekend at Bernie's* is showing."

"What?"

"At the drive-in. We could go down tomorrow."

I know he was trying to make everything seem so small that it would pass like an afternoon breeze. I guess it was kinda my fault.

I wasn't giving him the full story and I wasn't ready to now. "You ain't helping, Tiki. Go home," I said. The mask fell, and I could see his face drop. I immediately felt sorry for dismissing him like that.

When I went inside, Sam and Mr. Moonesar was sitting at the kitchen table. Moonesar was the only one to tell me good evening. Sam just grunted, got up and pull up a chair. I sat down and looked at them for a while. I'm not sure if they was waiting for me to say something. So I began, "Let me explain—"

Sam cut me off, "The good man here already tell me everything."

"No, well, lemme give you my side of it."

Sam shook his head. "You assault a girl and then run away like a coward—that is your side of it?"

You know, at that moment, I thought I woulda feel bad. But I was more angry than anything. Just because Sam had no control of Nick didn't mean he had to beat me down with a sledgehammer. Still, I try my best to remain calm. "That is not the full story," I said.

"The full story, my ass. Lemme guess the full story. Girl come at you and you swing to knock she down. So none of it is your fault then?"

I was so mad then that I hit the table. "What I suppose to do? Take the lash and shut my mouth?"

Sam hit the table even harder. "Yes, Anjali, take the lash and walk away! Not knock nobody down!"

"Um," Moonesar said, adjusting his tie. But he didn't say anything after that.

"Moonesar wasn't even there to see what happen—"

"Um ... Hmmm ..." Moonesar's voice bumbling through.

Sam locked eyes with me. "So the man making up stories then?"

"I just saying that he need to hear the full story!" My fists was clenched.

Sam was unusually calm after that. "I don't care if the full story pave with unicorns and rainbows," he said. "At the conclusion of it was a beast you couldn't take hold of. And you end up damaging another person and then try to avoid all consequences. You wasn't raise to be like that."

"You know we don't tolerate that kind of thing, Ms. Mathura," Moonesar said to me. "So I've come to the decision to suspend you and Ms. Reese." I knew it was coming, but it was still a shock to hear it. I ain't never been suspended before.

"For a week," Sam said.

"For the rest of the week. It's Wednesday today. She can come back in on Monday."

"This Reese," Sam said. "This is Nidhan Reese child?"

Moonesar hesitated but finally answer, "Yes. Mr. Reese died a few years ago."

Sam leaned forward, his elbows on his knees. He looked like he was deep in thought, rattling his mind for details. "Yeah. He had blood sugar. Went blind, end up in a coma. He ain't leave much behind. I went to the wake over at the squatter settlement. I remember it."

Moonesar didn't say anything, just bowed his head.

Sam suddenly get up from his chair. "Thank you for coming by, Mr. Moonesar. Always appreciated." He reach out his hand to shake Moonesar's—the conversation was over. After Moonesar drove off Sam turned to me and said, "We goin to handle this right now."

"Handle what?" It was only after I see Sam putting on his cap I realized what he meant. He wanted to walk me down to the shantytown to apologize to Alma.

I took a deep breath, didn't fight it. If it meant squashing the whole thing, so be it.

It was only a ten-minute walk, and it was still bright out when we arrived. At the front was a heap of garbage—plastic bottles and waterlogged plywood—where a pack of stray dogs sat. They raised their ears at us as we walked by. Sam remembered the house. It wasn't so much a house as it was a wooden shack surrounded by tall grass. There was no fence or gate. A clothesline ran from the light pole to the windowsill. They was using a bedsheet as a curtain.

Sam pointed to the door and gestured for me to lead the way. I looked at him like he was mad, but his expression didn't change. So, I went up to the door and knock on it. I closed my eyes, hoping no one would answer. Or at least that Alma wasn't home.

The door opened. "Yeah?" A woman stood before me, tapping her long, muddy nails against the doorframe. She had more lines on her face than a walnut, but behind them I coulda see her resemblance to Alma. She was barefoot and wearing a nightie that was too small for her.

Sam step forward, taking off his cap. "Your daughter and my granddaughter had a little altercation today," he said.

She twist her mouth. "Alter-what?"

"A fight."

She looked behind her. "Yeah. The school already say. I takin care of it."

"My granddaughter here wanted to apologize." I had to hold back a scoff when Sam said that. *Wanted to apologize*, what a joke.

The woman narrow her eyes at me. "It was a man allyuh was fightin over?" I shook my head, still couldn't say nothing. The woman then raise her eyes to the sky and shriek out, "Alma!" She didn't even turn around to do it.

There was no answer. She do it again. "Answer me, girl! Almaaa!"

Still no answer. Sam looked like he was starting to realize this wasn't a good idea. He put his cap back on and gave her a smile and said, "She probably sleepin."

"She better be sleepin!" The woman was about to pop a vein. She storm off into the back and near damn kick the door down. Alma was belly-down on the floor, flipping through a magazine. "You wasn't hearin me, girl?"

"I was comin," Alma said, getting up. As she stood up, she noticed me and Sam at the door and froze.

"How you have this room so?" the mother said, picking some clothes up from the floor.

"Stop cleanin up," Alma tell her, suddenly annoyed.

"Look at all this shit you have all over." Her mother was still picking up magazines and saucers and snack packs.

Alma saw me watching. "What the hell you lookin at?" she barked at me.

The thing is, I didn't care. But that didn't matter. I guess, she had it in her mind that people was always watching, always judging. Maybe I did have something to apologize for. I come to realize hitting Alma with my bag wasn't the most painful thing I do to her. I dunno if she can still hear that laughter from that Carnival Monday. You never know what impact you gonna have on somebody, no matter how small you feel your actions are.

Alma turned to her mother. "Ma, you hard of hearin? Stop cleanin up!"

"How you could live like this, eh? No respect for youself. Only want to fight over man."

Alma was fuming now. "I don't need to fight over no man. At least I have a man."

Her mother dropped everything she had been picking up. They watched each other like two grimacing dogs, one waiting for the other to make a move. Alma's mother was first. She grab a belt that was hang up on a nail and yell out, "So you talk to your mother, you lil bitch?"

And the woman started whipping like she was crazy. She

was whipping with the buckle too. Alma started scrambling out the door but her mother grab her by the hair before she could get out.

I turned around and was already walking away. But Sam was still watching, like he was shell-shocked by the whole thing. I went back to him only to hear him muttering to himself, "Stop that. Don't do that." It was like he was trying to ask a tornado to stop. I didn't want to look, but I coulda hear the floor shaking and Alma crying out.

I tugged on Sam's sleeve but he pull away, suddenly making a grand charge into the house. I looked around to see if anybody was coming out of their house, but there was nobody. I looked over to Sam. He wrap himself around the mother and was trying to yank her off. He pulled and pulled and pulled. Then he fell backwards, the woman plummeting down with him.

I rush in as soon as that happen. I heard something crack and Sam let out a deep wheeze. I thought the worst at first—that he was getting a heart attack. But it wasn't that. The woman land square on his nose, breaking it. Two lines of blood was trailing down from his right nostril to his chin. A dark crescent of blood on the bridge of his nose.

I was in a frenzy after that, running to every corner looking for a tissue or cloth. Alma and her mother was on the ground, just watching. Sam held his hand up to me as if telling me to stop. He took a rag out of his pocket and wipe his face. "Is nothing, Rune. Is nothing," he said, pinching the rag over his nose bridge. He didn't say nothing to the other two.

Sam walked home just like that, his neck tilted back, rag pressed against his nose. As we passed the stray dogs, he turned to me and said, "Not all of them's like that."

When we got home, Sam flop down on the recliner. I went to get Das who wasted a good minute staring at it before doing anything. Together we ice it, and Das snap it back into place. Sam gave Das the instructions. Das was more nervous than Sam, it seem. As for me, I couldn't watch. At the end of the whole thing, Sam had a giant bandage creeping from cheek to cheek. "What you goin to tell people?" Das asked him.

"Exactly what happen," he said, grinning. "A lady was on top of me and she was too rough."

CHAPTER 19

PIGS HAVE TEETH?

The next day, the sun ain't bother to show its face. But it didn't look like it set up to rain either. It was just dark. Something about it—made me feel like I was in a different world. Maybe I was. On my way to the pig farm, I stopped on the track to gaze at the cows. Kept my eyes on them, each one in its own corner. I remember wishing that one would come up to me. I probably waited for ten minutes to see if they would. But they was in a world of their own, just like me.

The beginning of the afternoon went on like normal. Me and Baram, we clean the pens, spread the new hay. I coulda tell Baram's mood was off. He kept a distance from me. I wondered if it had anything to do with Joey. He ain't crack no stale jokes, ain't ask how my day was. He wasn't in his rocking chair when I meet him. He ain't even ask if I was thirsty. It was like he was a different person.

He was at the far corner of the yard, raking and bagging foliage and weeds, a cigarette stub hanging from his lips, almost smoked to the filter. A radio was playing from a dirty wood pedestal near the pens, a man rambling on about whatever. I lowered the volume—I couldn't take it. I had a headache.

I paced up and down the pens, making sure all of them was clean. In the yard, Hara the stud was by himself. He sat in the corner, in the shade, hunch up, blinking his big wet eyes at me. I went up to him, slow and careful like I was on a tightrope, and put my hand out. I remember thinking at the time that his mouth was big enough to bite my arm clean off. But I wasn't scared.

He came up to me and push his snout against my hand. Like he coulda tell my mood was off. I brushed the bridge between his eyes. This sudden feeling of falling come upon me and I wanted to throw my hands around his thick bulbous neck. Like I just wanted something to hold on to.

He scraped the ground with his feet. It had something stuck to them.

I bent down to take a look and reach my fingers between his toes and plucked out two white thorns. But when I took a closer look—I realized they wasn't thorns.

They was teeth. Human teeth. A molar and a canine.

"Let's get them pigs back in," Baram's voice from behind me.

I shoved the teeth into my pocket, surprising myself how good I was keeping myself together in this bizarre situation—tying and untying the tethers, walking the pigs, spreading the feed. I was just counting down the minutes till I could get the hell outta there.

When we was done, he offer me a drop home. I told him I had my bike and that I didn't need to trouble him. He didn't fight me. He looked at me again for a long time, then gave me a small nod. I tried not to walk away too fast. My legs was fighting my brain, is how I could put it. But as soon as I got on my bike, there was no stopping. I ain't even bother roll it down the muddy track. I just rode like hell.

I rode all the way past the village and to the drive-in, where Tiki said he was going to be. I found him, sitting on our hill, the radio next to him. And there he was, on the grass in his good jeans. I parked the bike next to him. "Look who still breathing," he said, scooting to the side. I didn't realize how fast my heart was beating till I plop down next to him.

I took in a minute of the movie playing on the screen. A party in a big white people house, everyone trying to talk to this mustached man slump over on a couch. He had on shades, limp like he was dead. I asked Tiki, "What the hell is this you watching?"

"*Weekend at Bernie's.*"

"What going on with the man on the couch?"

"He dead."

"And nobody care?"

"Nobody want to care."

"How he dead?"

He shrugged. "It matter?"

We sat and watched for a few more minutes. I was searching my head to find the words—how I was going to tell Tiki about the teeth. I decided to just show him. I reached into my pocket and took them out. "Look at these," I tell him.

"What's that?" He leaned over. "Teeth? Who teeth is that?"

"I dunno."

"You dunno? So what you doin with it?"

"I find them at the farm. Today—in a pen."

"Pigs have teeth?"

"These look like human teeth, Tiki."

He turned the radio down. "This some kinda joke?"

"You're the only person I show this to."

"This is for real?"

"Don't—"

"Don't worry, I not goin to tell nobody. But why it have teeth in the pig pen?"

I scratched the back of my head. I took a while to answer. I think it was hard for me to really grasp the horror of the situation. "The man who run the farm—Baram is his name. He was joking around the day before about feeding people to pigs."

"What you mean, feeding people? Pigs eat people?"

"It coulda be a joke, I dunno."

Tiki paused. "What's the name of this place again?"

"Sty Trail Farm."

"You have to go back, or you done?"

"Tomorrow is my last day."

He cock his head. "You ain't stupid enough to go back, right?" I put the teeth back in my pocket and pull my knees up to my belly. Tiki lean in closer. "Rune, don't be crazy."

"Might look suspicious," I said.

"Suspicious how?" he asked. "If you don't go?"

"Yeah." He throw his hands up and gave me a look like I really was crazy. I was starting to think that maybe I really was crazy. Part of me wanted to see if the nightmare was true. What was gonna come after that—I dunno. But I didn't want to be left wondering. I wanted the whole thing to be a big misunderstanding. Just like with Lambi and Duster. I said to Tiki, "I just gonna be in and out, promise. Do what I have to do and get out."

"Just say you sick. You eat a bad curry. You step on a rusty nail. Shit, you might as well step on a rusty nail than go back there!"

"Stop it, Tiki." I took a deep breath. I was glad I didn't even mention seeing Joey's car. "Where you going to be tomorrow after school?" I asked him.

"The car yard."

"Then I'll check you at the yard tomorrow. As soon as I'm done."

"Rune, just do what you have to do and get out."

"In and out and done."

CHAPTER 20

EVERYBODY MAKE DECISIONS THEY AIN'T PROUD OF.

I n and out and done. I kept the words in mind. I took my raincoat with me. The sky was set up and the clouds was black-black, like coals from a barbecue. Every once in a while, the sunlight would crack through. The day was so cold that the light feel like velvet against my skin.

When I got to the farm, the first thing I noticed was that the cows wasn't there. Can't explain why but that was when the worry start to settle in. A big part of me wasn't accepting the situation. I thought back to how nice Baram was to me. I didn't want to be scared of the man, but I was trembling every moment I was near him. Couldn't help it. My brain wasn't scared but my body was. My hands was fumbling like crazy as I spread the last of the feed. Any opportunity I coulda get, I sifted through the clumps of hay for anything out of the ordinary. Another tooth. A chipped bone. Human hair. But nothing.

While we was leading the pigs back in, I asked to use the bathroom. I didn't really need to go but I needed a space to catch my breath, stop my mind from racing. He hesitated but told me to go right in.

So I went. I ain't realize how dead tired I looked till I saw myself in the bathroom mirror, looking like I just crawl out of a grenade explosion. As I washed my face, the reddish stain under the sink caught my eye. Blood. Rust. I don't know.

When I came out, I noticed a room I ain't see before. The door had always been shut. Looked like it was his bedroom. Inside, the bedside drawer was slightly ajar. I crept in and pulled it open.

My heart jump—there was a gun.

Next to it was a brown paper bag, like the ones you get prasad in. I took it out of the drawer.

"Shit!" I hiss out as I open it.

It fall to the floor and about a dozen teeth spilled out.

I just stood there like God sap all the sense outta me. My

muscles was stone. I had to break outta the daze fast. Teeth was all over the floor—by the fan, under the bed, everywhere. I fell to my knees, scrambling to pick them up and put them back in the bag. I didn't know how many there was—didn't see how many fell. I swept my hand under the bed, across the muck and grime. I couldn't reach.

At the same time, I was hearing footsteps. Baram was on the porch. When he walked, the whole house shook. "Come, gal, we hafta finish up," he called out, opening the front door.

There was no time. It was down to seconds.

I crumpled the bag, stuck it in the drawer and darted right out the room. I couldn't remember if I shut the drawer. There was teeth still under the bed, I knew it. Baram came up to me, his eyes cutting through me. That was when it full-on hit me, when I accepted it. The nightmare was real. Baram was feeding bodies to the pigs. Bodies that Joey created. I dunno why he was doing it. I thought back to all them blood-soaked car trunks at the yard and what Tiki said. Maybe Baram didn't cut up the bodies himself. Maybe he just let Joey use the farm to do it. He couldn't even make a slice in that little girl's throat to save her life—he was gonna do this?

Maybe he thought it woulda been a one-time thing and did it only because he needed the money. You just had to do something once for Joey and you was in it for life, it seem. I suppose the why didn't matter past that point.

I coulda believe all of that at that point. But no matter how good of a person Baram might've been before, no matter if he was hacking up the bodies himself or if Joey was doing it. He was a part of what is evil, now—bones crunched like bread, blood lapped up like milk. And I was helping him clean it all up.

"How you lookin so?" he asked.

I was sweating like a madwoman, hair tussled, crazy like a sprayed cockroach. I didn't know what to say. I didn't have a plan. "I think I coming down with a fever." That was the best I coulda come up with. "I should start getting home."

He peered over at the bedroom door. It was still open. He shut the door, leaning against it. I couldn't read his look—but he wasn't taking his eyes off me. At that moment, I coulda hear everything. The birds fluttering from the roof. The thunder in the distance. The grunting from the pens. My eyes veered over to the pyjama pants on the wall.

My feet was hard against the floor—I was ready to jump.

"You's not no bad child," Baram finally spoke. "Probably make bad decisions, but not a bad child." I wasn't sure where he was going with this. It gave me chills, I ain't gonna lie. He continued, "I ain't want to hear bout you sneakin in on nobody property again, hear me?"

I gave him a nod. I couldn't open my mouth to say nothing.

He said, laughing, "Sneak into this place and I goin to keep you lock up in a pig pen for a few days."

"Not going to happen," was all I could muster out. "I better start heading home."

"Yup," he said, his gaze going right through me. At the same time, the rain come down. "Could give you a drop if you want," he offered.

"I'm good," I said, getting my raincoat, slinging it around my back. Felt like it took all my energy just to walk out the house. I wasn't home free yet and the rain was really lashing down by then.

As I was about to get on my bike, he called out, "Wolfgirl!"

My shoulders nearly jump off my body. I froze. Felt all my bones shatter as I turned around to watch him. He said, "Everybody make decisions they ain't proud of. That don't mean they bad. This was a good week for me. You was good company."

I gave him a nod. And I was off.

CHAPTER 21

THE STATE I WAS IN, I WAS READY FOR ANYTHING.

The rain was pelting like bullets, so much and so hard that everything looked white in the distance. Was like the whole world disappeared except the road ahead. My head was spinning. I was still on Old Trunk Road, already half a mile away from the pig farm but I wasn't home free—I kept turning around to see if I was being followed. The rain beat my face, cold and stinging like acid. Every pitch of thunder aiming to fling me off my bike.

A burst of white flash from the sky. God was angry.

I lost my bearings for a little while. I wasn't even sure if I was on the road anymore. I had my eyes to the sky, looking out for another burst of lightning before I felt my whole body shift as a great force knock me onto the asphalt. A loud burning screech tore through the downpour.

I fell flat on my face. Pain shooting up my teeth and down my neck.

Couldn't get up, was like a boulder crushing me. Tried to wiggle my fingers—each one feeling like it had seeds rattling in the bones. Like my hands was maracas.

I felt like time was skipping. I wasn't sure if a second or half hour had pass before the road came into view. Then I saw it—what hit me.

Buick Regal. Cream-coloured hood. Mahogany brown roof. The car was at a right angle to the road, trunk flown open, trail of red leaking out. Windshield wipers going *screak-screak*.

As I curled my knees to prop myself up, lightning cracked the sky again. The driver's door was open. But I couldn't see nobody. I had a feeling Joey wasn't gonna help me up this time. I was expecting anything at that moment. For the engine to jump out at me. For a human head to come rolling out. The state I was in, I was ready for *anything*.

I stood up in the middle of the road, making sure I could

balance before I took a step. The reflector from my BMX had broke off. It was in the middle of the road while the rest of my bike was nowhere to be seen. I pulled the raincoat hood over my head, stumbling around, searching for the bike. There was a gully at the side of the road, down a slope, behind some sedges. I went to the edge and looked down where the water was gushing a butterscotch brown.

I saw two figures down in it. Two men. One standing, one in the water. The tall bushes towering behind them.

I got on my knees, leaning to get a closer look. The one standing—I knew it was Joey from the slouch. The way it made his silhouette look headless. He looked up, right at me. But I wasn't sure if he really saw me. I couldn't see his face so I don't think he coulda see mine. We was just blurry shadows to each other in the downpour. I scuttled to the other side of the road, into a cane thicket. My raincoat hooked onto one of the stems, nearly ripping it right open. I fell on my side, grazed my elbow. A yelp flew out my mouth, but I think the rain drowned it out.

I couldn't see much from where I was, crouched down in the cane. Couldn't hear nothing through the downpour either. Kept my feet sturdy against the soil. I kept backing up, backing up.

Then I saw Joey—not Joey himself but I saw the leaves shifting, the cane stalks bending and snapping as he got closer and closer. I curled up into a tight ball, hands tucked into my armpits, wrists stiff from the pain.

I pulled the hood tight over my face as I saw his hand, inches away, parting the cane stalks. The cold wind seep in.

I put my hand in the dirt and scooped up a glob of mud.

He pushed his face through. I saw his red eyes before anything else. The middle of his face was streaked with mud. I was right in front of him, so obvious that he had to do a double take to make sure I was real.

At the same time, I slammed my hand against his nose—
squish!—and he let out a loud, bubbling grunt, staggering backwards.
Wasn't sure if he fell as I was already gone. I cut through the cane,
back to the road. I didn't know what I was going to do. No plan. My
body was making all the decisions.

I darted back to the gully, eyes dashing back and forth to find
my BMX. I didn't know if it was still in one piece. I didn't even know
if it was in the gully. My brain finally pulled through—telling me:
Forget the bike. Run!

I turned around and Joey was just a few steps away. He was
like a shadow in the white rain. He had his hand outstretched.

In the blur of the rain, the gun was sharp and clear.

I bit down on my tongue till I tasted blood. My heart was
paining as if a bee slip its stinger into it. The pain creep all the way
to my wrists as I clenched them. I saw the flash. The shot barely
made a sound in the downpour—it was like a cherry bomb. The ring
of smoke almost instantly disappeared in the mist.

I skated down into the gully. My face landed right next to the
other man.

Half of his face was in the water. Water gushing into his
nose. A bullet hole through the side of his eye. The skin around it
grey and crumpled like paper. The body must have flown outta the
trunk when the Buick swerved.

My body started to spasm, like someone run jumper cables
into it. I clapped my palm over my mouth though even if I wanted
to scream, I couldn't. My tongue was heavy like a whale.

Between the gully and the road was a gradual incline of mud.
I ran along the incline, making zig-zags, slowly making my way
back up to the road. I didn't turn around but I knew I couldn't keep
on the road. I had to try to lose him in the cane so I took off into the
field, towards a row of transmission towers in the distance, looking
like metal church steeples smothered in fog.

I kept home on my mind the entire time. There was no other goal but home. The headache came back at full blast. I had to concentrate. Past the transmission towers was another stretch of road that I knew led back to the village. So I took off and ran till my legs burned. By the time I got back to the village, the rain began to calm down and the clouds broke apart into tight braids of purple.

NIGHT OF THE BEAST

CHAPTER 22

EVEN AFTER ALL OF THE NONSENSE, IT HAVE PEACE.

S am and Boss Das was in the yard when I got home. As I took the raincoat off, I saw the swept up glass shards. "Some lil hooligans pelt a big stone right through the blasted window," Sam tell me. It was only then I noticed the broken window. Whatever anger he had, it sound like it had fumed out by then. It was only after he said so I realized it didn't cross my mind to ask what happened. It ain't cross my mind to say anything—not even to tell them I was just chased and shot at.

"Two girls. They run up that way," Das said, pointing up the road. "To the squatters and them. Think they was squatter children, Sam? They break your nose and now they break your window."

Sam threw his arms up. "We dunno if it was the squatters, Das."

Das nodded. "This village goin to hell in a handbasket. How much a window cost, Sammy? You hafta make them pay back for it."

At the same time, Zandolee came pacing up from the corner. Sam called him out, "Aye! Aye, man! You up and down in this road every evenin. You see who do this?"

"Maybe," he said, scratching his head. "Maybe not. How much you payin?"

"Pay?" Sam sucked his teeth. "Man, git your ass outta here."

Das said, "Tellin you, Sammy. They went up to the squatter settlement."

"I ain't think it was no squatter children. What reason they would have for doin this? Nobody have anything against—" then Sam paused, shaking his head. He muttered out, "This is that damn boy fault, you know."

"Who?" Das asked.

Sam didn't reply, but I knew he was talking about Nick. He probably thought Rita and Salaman did this.

"Things like this, you have to take care of it early," Das said. "You sure you ain't want to call the police?"

"Bah. What they could do?" Sam flicked his hand. "News startin."

We all went inside. Sam went on the recliner, me on the floor. The news headlines started to play out. But there was nothing about a killing. I wondered if the body was still there. Gnats and midges chewing away on the neck. Halo of corbeaux overhead. Nobody ever really walked Old Trunk Road. The only type of person who coulda stumble across it was a bottle-collecting vagrant.

I didn't know what to think of that—that I knew a dead man was out there. The body was still there, I was sure.

When the news was done and Boss Das went back to his house, Sam put *Jai Santoshi Maa* into the VHS. My mind was racing again, replaying the crash, the gunshot, the body. I wish I coulda find some kinda fuse to blow in my head to shut my mind off. I concentrated on the actors, their painted skin, the movie sets built to look like the heavens, some sitting on glowing lotus petals, some floating in never-ending space.

"You see this in the movie house, you know," Sam said, looking down at me on the floor. "Bet you didn't know that."

I shook my head. "I can't remember."

"Course you can't remember." He laugh. "You was two years old. Your mama had you in a blanket. That girl went everywhere with you. She coulda leave you with me, but she use to ride down in a bicycle and sneak you in even though she didn't have to. Is she who pass down the mischief and fire to you, I know it."

I kept shaking my head.

He turned to me. "Tell you, she take you everywhere—wrap up in that umber-brown blanket. Is okay if you don't remember." His voice had that scratchy sadness in it. His eyes went back to the screen.

"Satyavati," he muttered after a while, turning to me again. "The main character in this movie, her name is Satyavati. She have some sisters-in-law there, real wicked girls. Always beating she. And she always have to be rescue by this god name Santoshi Maa. Was supposed to have this ceremony for Santoshi Maa near the end of the movie. But the sister-in-law characters mess it up. Santoshi Maa, she watch straight into the camera and the earth start to shake, eyes flashing like red lights. You see volcanoes eruptin, lightnin cuttin the sky, wind throwin pillars down."

He paused, took a breath and finish, "But at the end, she return all to peace. Even after all of the nonsense, it have peace. I like to think of that. Even after war, it could have peace."

Part of me liked that, found comfort in it—even if it was only a movie. Sam fell asleep in his recliner not too long after that. I turned the TV off and he woke up. But he was just zombie-awake. He patted my head and went straight to his room. I stayed there, sitting in the silence, watching my reflection on the dark screen. Everything just seemed like a dream. I think I just wanted it to be. Might sound strange, but realizing what Baram had got himself in— that was worse than the body and the gunshot. People talk about moments where you know your life was never going to be the same. You take a while to accept it.

This was it. I just wasn't realizing it yet.

CHAPTER 23

FOR ARUNDHATI. KEEP YOUR BALANCE, KEEP MOVING! — SAM.

There was a knock at the door and then the window. I braced myself, expecting the window to shatter, expecting a rock to come zipping through into the living room. But when I got up to look, I saw Tiki. He was panting like he just run a marathon. I went to the door.

He was beckoning for me to come out. So I did, closing the door behind me. "Sty Trail Farm," he muttered out. "That's where you was, right?"

"Yeah—"

Then he pulled a piece of paper out of his pocket and unfolded it. I recognized it immediately. It was a flyer for the farm, with that ridiculous pig. Before I could ask him what he was doing with this, he say, "Joey bring his car into the yard this evening. And I find this in the backseat."

At that moment I feel like I coulda step outside my body and see myself. My face ghost-white. Tiki continued, "Had blood in the trunk. Rune, if what you say about the pig farm is true—"

"I saw him," I spat out. Slower now, "Joey. I saw the body."

His jaw dropped. "You see it? At the farm?"

"No, not at the farm," I said. "Unless he went back for it."

He crinkled his brow. "Went back for it? Where you see the body then?"

"In a gully. Along Old Trunk Road—coming back from the farm. Joey run right into me. I was on my bike. The body fall out the trunk—"

Tiki looked me dead in the eye. "He didn't see you, right?"

I hesitated. "I dunno. It was raining like crazy. My face was covered." I didn't want to tell him about the gunshot. "My bike's still there—" I froze up, remembering my previous encounter with Joey. When he had nearly knock me over as we was coming back from the poultry farm. The way his eyes scanned me and my bike. He even said, *That's a nice BMX.* Then the other words shot across my mind:

> For Arundhati. Keep your balance, keep moving! – Sam.

The card on the wheel. The card Sam had pegged to the spoke. My name was right there. Mine and Sam's.

"Shit!" I hiss out before turning to Tiki. "We have to go back now."

Tiki took a step back. "Where?"

"My bike's still there. It was raining so hard I couldn't find it. My bike is still where the body is—"

"That's all right. Everybody have a BMX—"

"No, no, no. My name is on it, Tiki."

"Shit." He clenched his teeth.

My feet wanted to run right out from my hip. "We have to go get it," was all I said.

"It could ride?" he asked.

"Shit. Not sure." Truth was that it was probably wrecked. Even if we found it, I dunno how we was gonna get it back here.

Tiki drew a deep breath, deep in contemplation. "It have a way," he finally said, putting his hand on my shoulder. "But we have to be real careful, understand?"

"We can't waste time, Tiki."

"Then let's go."

I didn't realize what the plan was till we got to the car yard. There was a Toyota pickup in the shadow of the shed. Tiki slid a piece of metal under its window and propped the door open. He tell me to keep a lookout while he fiddled with the wires on the driver's side, a flashlight in his mouth. I thought back to our conversation near the drive-in, how he warned me. I was thankful he didn't fling it back in my face. Still didn't stop me from feeling bad.

"Tiki, I shoulda listen. I'm sorry—"

"We have to do what we have to do," was all he said, still fiddling. "Don't worry. I do this already."

He was right. There wasn't no alternative. We had to get that bike back. I knew there was a chance all of this woulda be in vain—so many things coulda gone wrong already. Joey coulda already be at my house for all I knew. But there was a chance, even if it was a small sprinkle of one, that we could actually pull through. And I could save myself. No gods was coming down to do it.

Tiki finally get the pickup started. "Veni vidi vici," he said. He had this proud smirk on his face as if he forgot why we was even here in the first place.

"The body," Tiki said as we was pulling out of the yard. "You recognize it?"

I shook my head. "No. Was just some man."

"I wonder what he did."

"It don't matter now," I said, turning the radio on. That 'More Than Words' song was on—I didn't really like the song. But I needed something in the background to take away the tension.

The road was bumpy, splotched with puddles. Each car that went past sent a wave of heat down my stomach. It was dark and the air was hot. "Drive slow," I said to Tiki as we got to the road with the gully. Everything looked different at night. I couldn't make out the spot where the accident had occur. There was no landmark or nothing like that. Just a mile of road and a mile of gully next to it.

The car slowed to a crawl, the engine rumbling so low that I could hear the crickets. "You think we could smell it?" Tiki asked.

"I doubt it," I said, shaking my head. "It was still looking fresh."

Up ahead was a tiny light flashing at us from the road. As we got closer, I realized it was the reflector from my bike. "Right here, right here," I kept saying, motioning for Tiki to stop the car and kill the headlights. He did, leaving the engine running.

"You gonna look?" he asked, the flashlight in his hand.

My hands began to shake as I took it from him. I got out of the car and shone it down into the gully. I nearly dropped the flashlight when I saw it, still facedown in the water, torso twisted to the side, one arm folded over the chest, the other pointing to the road. Skin the colour of old mayonnaise. Flies, rainwater and muck.

Tiki was right behind me. I can't describe the look on his face—eager but pale like death at the same time. It was that horror house kinda feeling. He shifted closer to the sedges, peering right down. He couldn't muster up any words except, "I never see a real one before, you know."

"Me neither," I replied.

"We just leaving it here?" he asked, still hypnotized by the sight.

"You ain't suggesting that we put it in the pickup?"

"We have to tell somebody at least."

Tiki was right. Nobody in their right mind would feel comfortable knowing a murdered body was lying round somewhere and not say anything. I mean—that's partially how I end up on the pig farm in the first place. But we had to be smart and make sure we was in the clear first. It had to be all in its own time.

"Tiki, we have to find the bike," I said. That was the number one priority. I shone the flashlight up and down the gully but the BMX was nowhere to be seen. It had to be here, I kept telling myself—it couldn't have gone far.

Unless it was already gone.

"Someone comin'!" Tiki hissed. I looked out in the distance. Two headlights. "Back in the truck. Go!"

We pelted back into the pickup—me in the driver's side, Tiki in the passenger's, both of us ducking down as if we was about to take shelter from gunfire. The lights hit us, beaming right on us like we was centre stage. The vehicle had stopped. No sound but the low growls of our engines vibrating in unison.

"What happening out there?" I whisper.

Tiki ain't reply. A shiver ran down my spine. I had a feeling that this was it. The reaper had come to collect, come to clean up. And we was stuck in the middle of the business. "Tiki, what's the plan?" I tried not to sound scared, but I was one jolt away from pissing myself.

Tiki stayed quiet. Whatever was gonna go down, it was going to come down to the second. At the same time, I remembered a story Sam was telling about two friends running from a grizzly bear. Survival of the fittest. If you don't want to get eaten, you ain't have to be faster than the bear, he said. You just have to be faster than your friend.

But I wasn't going nowhere without Tiki. If Tiki wasn't running, I wasn't.

I heard the doors of the other vehicle open and close. Mumbling came from outside—two men.

I looked up at the window on the passenger side. A shadowy face was peeking in.

"Look, is these two!" the man said.

"Little shits!" the other bawl out.

The door flew open and a hand reached, wrenched Tiki out. I screamed.

At the same time, the door on my side yanked open and a hand grabbed my shoulder. I tried to beat the man off—but he jerked me right out of the seat. They dragged Tiki into the light. At the same time, I noticed the car. Ford Fiesta.

Then the men. Raja and Nick. I can't even describe the relief that wash down on me. I looked over at Tiki. The boy beaming like he wanted to laugh through all the commotion.

"You springing cars now, boy?" Raja said. "You thought you coulda get away?"

"Rune, you all right?" Nick said, rum on his breath. "What you doin here? You dunno what could happen to you?"

Raja was about to pop a vein. He asked again, "You thought

you coulda get away?"

Tiki was still chuckling out of sheer relief. "We was just borrowing it. I didn't think anybody woulda notice."

"You was on the cameras," Nick tell me.

Raja grabbed Tiki's collar. "I didn't know you was a thief like your girlfriend."

Tiki just gave him a shrug. I could tell Raja was trying to rile him up, but Tiki wasn't having it. But his patience didn't last for long. Raja gave Tiki a big smile. "I goin to tell your father bout this, loverboy."

Tiki's face drooped almost immediately. It began to twitch like there was ants crawling down his nose. Raja started to laugh when he saw this reaction. Tiki let out, "Anything happen to the car? You seein any dents, scratches? No, nothing. You know what my father would do, so you better shut your mouth."

"Uncle gonna fix you up good when you reach home," Raja said, still laughing.

I stepped up. "Raja, shut your mouth."

"Don't play like you walkin up to me, thief."

"Ease up, Raja," Nick said, putting his hand on his shoulder.

Raja gave me a shove. It was a play shove, probably mean nothing, but Tiki, he jump in, automatic, and shoved Raja back so hard he nearly toppled over. Tiki wasn't playing. And Raja wasn't anymore. "Both of you, stop it!" I yelled as they got closer and closer to the edge of the road.

At the same time, Nick leapt in to stop it—at least I think he did. Tiki ended up shoving Nick right into the gully.

"Shit!" Raja said, looking down at Nick as he landed in the shallow water. "He get you good!"

Nick got up, rubbing his jaw, brushing the mud off his pants. I shone the flashlight on his dazed face. Raja got on his knees, as if to take a closer look. "Gimme that," he tell me, snatching the flashlight from me before I could even respond. He shone the light on Nick's feet.

He hollered out, "Shit! Nick, it have something by your foot! Get the hell outta there now!"

Nick peered down at his feet. When he saw the body, he floundered out of the gully like a fish trying to get out of an overturned bowl. When he got back up to the road, he spewed out a big curried blob of vomit. "Jeezus!" Raja cry out. "That is a dead body!"

I didn't know what to do. Tiki stepped forward. "I think this is the man Joey kill before he brought the car in."

Raja pointed in his face, hissing, "You better shut your mouth."

"I ain't lying, Raja."

"Joey?" Nick wiped his mouth, still hunch over, hands to his knees.

"We have to tell somebody," Tiki added.

"No, no, we have to think about this," Raja said, holding his head. He paced around, biting his nails.

I stood up straight. "We have to find the bike first. Then we could call it in. Anonymous."

"Who goin to do that?" Raja said, narrowing his eyes at me. "You? Your drunk ass brother?"

"I ain't messing round with no Joey Jodha, man," Nick said, holding his palms up.

Tiki asked, "So we just gonna pretend it don't have a dead body lying right there?"

"Nobody pretending nothing," I said. "We'll call it in later. We have to get the bike."

"Bike?" Nick asked, sounding sober all of a sudden.

"Somebody will call it in," Raja cut in, nodding. "Don't have to be we. You know what Joey goin to do if he find out bout this?

He will kill out we families and burn we houses down. Not me and that. I like my life. I like my house."

At the same time, Tiki pointed to the distance. Another pair of headlights was approaching. "Shit! Hide!" Raja hollered out.

But we was all too shook up to do anything. Nick bent over, looking like he was ready to heave again. I was paralyzed. Was like a whirlwind was coming and we couldn't do nothing about it.

Then the car stopped.

I couldn't even see the make of it—it was so dark. It flipped its lights to high-beam and sat there like it was a bull ready to charge. We stood facing it like gunslingers in an old western.

The door opened.

And that was it. Survival of the fittest. The bear and the friends.

Raja grabbed Tiki's arm and ran to the Fiesta. I couldn't see nothing else, it was so dark.

I ended up in the pickup with Nick. His foot trembling on the gas. We went one way. Raja and Tiki went the other. The mystery car was nowhere in sight. Either it was still parked there or it was long gone.

CHAPTER 24

YOU KNOW WHO I AM?
I'M THE WOODCUTTER.

I didn't have a clue where we was going. I suspect Nick didn't either. As grog up and frantic as he was, he was surprisingly sharp behind the wheel. Still, I had to keep one eye behind and one eye in front.

There wasn't time for questions. The brain can't process questions in situations like this. You just run—don't matter what direction. You just run. Eventually you find a light bulb to flutter towards. I was hoping that light bulb would be the police station. I know that some of them turned a blind eye to the bodies and the blood spatters and that some of them create them—but there was some good ones between the cracks. I felt like I coulda trust at least one. I was trying hard to remember her name. I turned to Nick. "Nick, something bad might happen if we don't tell somebody bout this."

"We don't have to tell nobody nothin. You ain't hear what Raja say?"

"Raja was exaggerating, right?"

"Raja would know Joey better than all of we. All I know is that if Joey comin after you, it might as well be the black plague. We don't need none of that." He looked at me. "Joey was a normal person once, you know. He wasn't much older than me or Raja. He used to build go-karts. He was just skin and bones, real religious. Used to get real licks from a couple of fellas. He get even more licks when his mother start comin in to complain. He real change after his mother die and he went to live with his father. Them fellas who used to bully him, they probably still drinkin food outta a tube. One by one, they drop like flies. He bring a gun to school once—just once. Never even had to point it. None of we dare tell a soul bout that."

I realized that Flambeau was just ahead in the distance. "Nick," I turned to him. "You know me and Tiki ain't find that body by accident, right?"

He shot a look at me. "What you mean?"

I took a deep breath. He had to know. Somebody had to know. "Earlier today, at that same spot, Joey nearly run me over. It was raining so hard, I guess he ain't see me. But as he dodge me, the body fly out of the trunk and right into the ravine."

Nick pulled over, this look of dread in his eyes. "He ain't see you, right?"

The moment he see me hesitate, his face cringe. I shook my head. "I ain't sure."

"What you mean, I ain't sure? He know you was there?"

"If what Raja say is true ... Nick, if Joey know it was we who was there and we don't tell the police, we good as dead."

"Shit!" He punch the steering wheel and the horn went off. As it did, the officer's name flash in my mind: Navarro. Nick leaned forward, taking a few seconds to calm down. He inched the car forward till Flambeau was almost in sight. "We in a real mess here."

"We need a plan," I said.

"Have a payphone in there." As he said that, a strange wave of relief wash over me, though the road ahead was swallowed by darkness. I couldn't even see no payphone. "But you never know with the police."

"Ask for Navarro," I tell him.

"What?"

"She's in the force. It would be safe to tell her."

He didn't respond. He got out of the car, leaving the engine running, and fiddled around his pockets for some change. "Stay here," he said as he left. I peered ahead at the darkness. Suddenly I felt like all the blood drain outta my head, like this sensation of doom creep into my head like a black widow spider.

"Nick, you know where you going?"

"Stay in the car," he said again. And he disappeared in the darkness.

I waited for five minutes. After that, I couldn't stay in the car any longer. I couldn't even sit. I kept pacing up and down the small length of road, tossing rocks into the bushes. I didn't want to be by myself. I kept gravitating towards Flambeau. Nobody coulda find me there, I thought. It was like I was seven years old all over again and afraid a jumbie in the night would reach out from under my bed and pull me down into hell.

I crept closer and closer to the Flambeau car park. A Dr. Hyde mixtape pumping loud and scratchy from one of the cars. A weatherbeaten Toyota Cressida. A girl sitting on the trunk, getting necked by what looked like an older boy. "Shit," I hissed, realizing who it was.

Alma.

I turned around and started walking right back to the car.

"You stalkin me, Rat?" She yelled out, drunk and slurring. "Come back here!" She leap off the trunk. The boy was looking in my direction now. He had this droopy caveman look. I wasn't sure if he was drunk too or if that was just how he looked.

I knew she wasn't going to go away, but I kept walking. I coulda see the pickup from where I was. Nick was still nowhere in sight. Halfway back to the pickup, I thought about running towards to the bar instead. Towards people, towards light.

I turned around right before I got to the pickup, and looked her square in the eye. The boy was behind her. He ain't seem to know what was going on but he looked like the type that coulda lick you down with the flat side of a cutlass. "Alma," I tell her. "Whatever we have, we could save it for another day."

She spit on the ground, slurring, "You feel you coulda just come in my house? Who you feel you is?"

"Alma, we need to squash this—me and you, it ain't need to be like this."

"You lookin to get your nose broke too?"

"Alma, I don't want to—"

And she pounce on me, hollering out like a hyena, laying blows on my face. I felt like I was being wrapped up in a tsunami. I wasn't even fighting back. I was just waiting for it to end.

It didn't last for long. After only a few seconds, I felt her being lifted off of me. And she went flying into the air, landing bottom-first on some gravel. At first I thought it was the boy who did it. But he was long gone. Everything was a blur. There was a man standing between us. I couldn't make out the man—was like he was carrying the darkness with him.

The man went over to Alma and lifted her up by the neck of her top. She kicked her feet like she was treading water. Only after the man stumbled back into the light, I see his face.

It was Joey.

Alma screwed up her face like it had caught fire and somebody beat it out with a shovel. I'm sure my face wasn't far from that either. I didn't understand what I was seeing. Seeing Joey here, I came to the realization that the mystery car back at the gully probably was nothing. Just a stranger on the road watching a couple of suspicious teenagers.

Joey looked Alma dead in the eye. "You know who I am? I'm the woodcutter."

"Let me go!" Alma grunt out. I was still on the ground, scooting a few paces back.

"You know the woodcutter from Red Riding Hood? How he cut open the wolf's belly and save the girl. The strong always want to eat the weak. But bullies have fake strength. I hate them more than I hate anything else. Hell not big enough for you people. You can still redeem yourself."

"Put me down!"

He hold her up higher. "Tell the girl you're sorry. Say it like a good girl." He was crushing her neck now.

Even through the pain, it took her almost half a minute to

say it.

As soon as Joey set her down, she scamper off back to the car park.

Joey looked down at me. I got up before he could offer to help. There was a small distance between us. He under the flickering streetlight, me in the darkness. I didn't budge. I wasn't sure if he recognized me. From either of our encounters. "It don't require much to get good people to fall in line with the rules," he tell me. "People who don't follow the rules from small ain't never going to follow the rules."

I didn't know what to do except nod.

"You're the girlfriend, right?" he asked. "What's your name?"

It took me a couple seconds to even lift my tongue. "We're just friends," I eventually tell him. His eyes was locked onto mine. Eyes like samurai steel. Was only then I realized I had shifted into the light.

"I asked your name."

"A-A-Anjali," I stammer out.

He nodded, then asked, "What you doing out here by yourself, Anjali?"

"Waiting for my brother."

"Your brother? Where is he? At the bar?"

"Um, making a call. The payphone."

"The payphone?"

"Y-Yeah."

"Why are you parked so far away from the phone?"

I swallowed the lump in my throat. "I dunno. I'm just waiting for him to come back."

He pulled out a cigarette from his shirt pocket and lit up. He blew the smoke into the darkness. At the same time, Nick returned. He paused, watching us, just an outline frozen against the darkness. "Look, that's him," I tell Joey. I ain't dare force a smile. "Thanks again for your help."

Joey put his hand on my shoulder. I steadied my breathing. "Your brother shouldn't be leaving you out here like that."

Nick came up to us. Joey turned to him and said, "I was just telling your sister that you never know what could happen nowadays. Storm could come, blow everything right away."

Nick forced a laugh. My heart was jackhammering. "We heading right home now," he say.

Just as Nick was about to open the door, Joey asked, "This your truck?"

"Um, a friend's," I answered for Nick.

He nodded. "I know a man with a pickup that look like this. Owns a pig farm not too far from here. You know who I'm talking about?"

My eyes shot to Nick and then back at Joey. "You asking me?"

He smiled, crumpling the cigarette in his fist, a fizzle of cinder push past the crimps of his index finger and thumb. "Yes. I'm asking you, Anjali."

I shook my head. "I don't think so."

"Never been up that side?"

"I can't remember."

"Big fat man—real hard to miss. Said he had a girl working for him for a few days. She was nice, he say. Rode a BMX."

He was just gauging my reactions now, playing with me. I crept closer to Nick, nudging his arm with mine.

"We have to go now," Nick said, almost robotic.

Joey's mouth twisted into a shark grin. "I know."

As we started walking back to the car, I held my breath, kept bracing for anything. I was half-expecting to be shot in the back. When we finally got back into the car, I coulda finally breathe. "We should go back to the car yard," I suggested.

"Best bet is back in the village," Nick said, hands clasped

on the steering wheel. It was a roll of the dice honestly. Joey was still watching us. I coulda see him in the side mirror. Nick had his eyes on him through the rearview. He was stalling. I drummed my fingers against the dashboard. I was so impatient.

"Let's get outta here," I tell him.

"What he was tellin you?" Nick asked, his eyes still on the rearview.

"It was nothing. Nick, let's go."

"I ain't like the way he was talkin."

"Me neither but come on—we have to go."

He finally drew his gaze to the front and stepped on the gas. The road was empty. It was just trees and bush at our side. The streetlights was flickering. We wasn't far from the village. Maybe five minutes. That was when I saw the car coming up from behind us. The Buick Regal, its lights on full-beam on us.

He began honking over and over. "Shit," Nick muttered, tightening his grip on the steering. "What the hell he doing?"

"Nick, just pull aside. Let him pass."

Then everything went dark. Power outage.

The Buick zoomed right past us. Nick swerved, fighting with the wheel. But we was already off the road.

The tyres were screeching like a banshee before the pickup pile slammed right into a tree.

CHAPTER 25
DON'T.

"**D**amnit, Nick!" He was out cold. No matter how much I shook him, he wasn't waking up. He had hit his head bad on the dashboard. The rum in his blood wasn't helping matters. I had to make a decision. I had to go get help.

I crawled out of the wreck and began my sprint back to the village. It wasn't far but there was nothing but a long stretch of road and bush. There was no light ahead but the moon. Everything was just shapes and angles. Phantoms and dust. I tried to keep Joey off my mind. The objective was to reach the village—nothing else. One thing at a time.

I made it back to Kukuyo. Everything was ghost-silent but the mosquitoes. You coulda barely even hear the crickets. The air was still, as if time had frozen. Like everybody in the village had got spirited away. Something was off. It cross my mind to just go banging on gates and asking for help but knowing how people in this place was—unless I was getting knifed to death in the dark street, nobody was coming out. So, I trudged towards Hallelujah Terrace, to Tiki's house.

I wasn't no stranger to the darkness. I know the sounds of the things that wasn't there, like they was seeping in from another world. The groans, pounding, hissing. But there was something else.

A *tuk ... tuk ... tuk ...* against the concrete, coming from behind me.

I spun around but couldn't see nothing. I started walking faster.

The sound sped up—*tuk! tuk! tuk!* It was getting closer—and I heard another sound faint-faint in the stillness. *Clink clink clink.*

I moved to sprint. But a force wrenched me down against the grit of the road. My arms against the asphalt. It felt like a boulder had fall on my knees. A line of drool began to puddle on my neck. I was facing up at the culprit but it was too dark to see anything. It was grunting—didn't even sound human. It was more like a rabid dog. Had this gasoline stench coming out from the skin.

I felt the thumbs on my neck, squeezing the air right outta my throat. I couldn't scream, couldn't breathe. The grip was too strong. I dragged my back along the road, the gravel cutting like fangs against my elbows. I kept kicking up, up, up.

A shout echoed from the distance. "Rune!"

The culprit toppled to the side, not even making a sound, and scuttled off into the darkness like a cockroach. There was footsteps running up to me, then a voice: "You hurt?" It was Nick, drained of breath. I couldn't see his face either, even after he pull me up.

"I'm good," I said, my hand over my heart.

"What the hell happen there?" He put his hand on my shoulder.

"I dunno." I began to ramble, "I was going to get help. It come outta the dark. It come outta nowhere—"

"Joey?"

I hesitated. "I dunno."

"Shit! Who else it woulda be, Rune?"

"Calm down, Nick. Okay?" I couldn't believe I had to be the one calming Nick down.

He suddenly went quiet. I couldn't tell at first but he was looking ahead at the sky. As I turned around, I saw it, as big as God— the orange glow in the distance, diffusing through the darkness. The fiery fork of light crawling above the roofs, just a few streets away. Shepherd Street. My mind tried to convince me that it was someone's backyard fire—foliage, garbage and kerosene. But it was too bright. The black corkscrew of smoke too thick.

Nick bust out in full speed. I couldn't catch up. People were coming out to their yard, some on the sidewalk. Some migrating towards the light. The rising soot was like black sutures from a hot wound. The heat. I'll never forget the smell—the dull stink filling the air. Dogs pawing the fences, dogs howling from their kennels.

On Shepherd Street, the ashes blew in the breeze like corbeau feathers.

The blaze looked like something out of a dream. Nick and I stood side by side before it, feet jammed to the asphalt, the muscles in my neck tensing up. A flock of people stood on the opposite side of the street. At the front was Boss Das and his wife. My eyes darting up and down the street. I counted and recounted the houses from each end.

I went up to Das. He threw his arms around me when he see me.

"Das, where is Sam?" Nick asked him.

Zandolee said, "Me ain't think he make it out, you know." He was swinging his arms, jolly like nothing was going on in the background.

I shot a look of dread at Das, and he let me go, averting his gaze to the ground. The women returned watery blinks to me. The others just looked away.

"You mean nobody in there tryin to get him?" Nick was frantic now.

I didn't even say a word. It was almost instinctive as I make a mad sprint towards the house. As I did, Das grabbed my shoulder. "Don't," was all he said.

I tore from his grip and barged into the fire. I heard a woman bawl as I did but the flames gulped the sound right down. Inside, the air was heavy and dark. Smoke everywhere. My eyes was ready to melt. I can't tell you I was being brave. The whole thing, it just didn't seem like it was really happening. The fire didn't seem real. It was like fantasy fire. Fire manufactured by some movie set. But the sting was closing in on me quick. A squirrel of fire scurry up the curtains as a loud crash sounded from the back.

The roof was collapsing. Walls was caving in.

I crawled, trying to breathe, breathe, *breathe*. Crawled all the way through the living room.

I caught a glance at the TV stand—the *Jai Santoshi Maa* jacket on the VHS. Sam's words resounding in my head. *Even after everything, there is peace.* I kept repeating the words as I slogged through the soot.

I eventually made it to Sam's bedroom's door. It was wrapped in flames. I couldn't even touch the knob. Couldn't get in. I just remember watching the door. I remember my breath. Nothing else. Everything slowed down, cranking down like a dying clock. I lost all sense of time. Maybe my mind block out the rest—but after that, it's all dark.

CHAPTER 26

THEY WAS JUST LOOKING FOR SOMETHING TO DESTROY.

I wasn't sure how long I was out. The first thing I saw was the fire truck—this big, red blur before everything else come into view. The giant snake of a hose splayed out on the road. The fire was dead. The ashes was still falling. Power was still out. The house wasn't a house no more. Each wall blotted black as if a cyclone of bats had pelted themselves headfirst into the concrete. The roof was clean gone, decapitated by the blaze. Grey dust clambering to the sky still. Glass like broken teeth. Not even a thread of curtain left.

Boss Das' house was only partially frayed—the trio of *jhandi* flags at the front of his house still lobbing firefly-like embers into the wind. Nick had my head in his lap, sitting cross-legged on the sidewalk. He was fanning me with an old dishcloth. He didn't even realize I had woke up. Even when I cough, he ain't pay no mind. He was gazing into the distance, as if he was in a trance.

Everybody else soon came into view. Women in their housedresses and muslin nightgowns, palms to their mouths, some holding their children against their bellies. The men stood straight, lips still tight with shock.

The only sound was the firemen. They was sitting in a row on the sidewalk, chattering like the teacher wasn't there. One of them was running back and forth, narrating an imaginary football game. "If you see how Dennis Bergkamp run that ball, boy! Dennis Bergkamp, they have wires and circuits in he, tellin you! Like *Terminator!*"

They reel the hose along the axle at the back of the truck before they shuffled back into it. One of them came up to us.

"Keep clear of the area in the meantime," he said. The man then turned to Nick. "The girl good?"

Nick didn't say anything—of course I wasn't good.

The fireman then looked at Das and said, "Ambulance coming just now." The firemen all went back on the truck, and it sped off, probably just as fast as it come.

It was only when they was gone, I saw what Nick was looking at. Joey was standing on the other side of the street, leaning against a lightpole, a smouldering cigarette dangling from his mouth. Joey arched his neck, puckered his lips and blow out a thick twine of grey.

Boss Das was looking at the house, shaking his head. "This ain't happen just so," he said to the crowd, waving his finger. "Somebody do this. You!" He point to Zandolee. "You always pacing up and down this blasted street—you musta see somethin! Every day I come home and see you wastin your blasted life watchin in people house."

The crowd parted around Zandolee. Zandolee let out a nervous chuckle. "Information like that don't come for free."

Das fired back, "You get drop on your head, boy?" He stepped up to Zandolee. The boy lifted his chin to the old man. Das grabbed him by his shirt collar and pulled him down eye-to-eye, growling, "If you know something, you better start talkin."

"Then I ain't know notten."

"The cockroach lyin!" Das' wife cut in. Nick was quiet the whole time, his eyes glued to Joey.

"Tell we what you see!" a voice yell out.

Another yell out, "He fraid to say! He ain't want he house to get burn down too!"

I tried wiggling my fingers at Nick to get his attention, but it felt like I couldn't even do that. My mind was sending the instruction but my body had shut right off. I felt so weak and disconnected that it was like one of them dreams where you're screaming and no sound could come out. "Nick," I was trying to say. "Make them stop."

"If the old man life was worth somethin, you would pay," Zandolee said.

Das looked like he was about to knock Zandolee right down.

At the same time, Nick got up from the sidewalk, putting me to lie on the concrete. He turned his head to the sky and cry out as if he was howling to the moon. Everything went quiet. All eyes shot to him. He raised a trembling finger, pointed it right at Joey and said, "Let him and his people strike me down, I ain't care! Look the culprit right there!"

All eyes shot to Joey. He flicked his cigarette into the drain. "Sit down, boy."

Nick shook his head. "I always know you was a crook and a menace, Joey Jodha. But I ain't afraid of you no more. Send people for me, shoot me dead and dump me in the ocean—I ain't care." He then turned to the crowd, saying, "Old Trunk Road, on the way to the pig farm have a dead body. You all can go check."

The crowd was creeping in on Joey. Their stiffened movements like the dead rising from the graves. I swallowed hard. I couldn't say anything. My throat was hurting so bad. I balled up my fists, blood rushing to my face, pins-and-needles on my mouth. Teeth chattering, I hawk and spit on the asphalt. My voice like burning wood crackling, "Nick, stop it."

But nobody was listening.

The crowd parted into two queues, Joey in the middle. All eyes jump to him. He was shaking his head. Everything went quiet. Ash still falling like black snow.

"That fool have no idea what he's talking about," Joey said to the crowd. "I come back from Flambeau only ten minutes ago. No way I burn that house down!"

At that same time, a stone—about the size of a corkball—come zipping across the crowd. It hit Joey square on the cheek. He didn't even make a sound—just wiped the blood away. A silence descended over the crowd at that moment. Even the dogs stopped barking. Joey had this metallic sharpness in his eyes. Whatever equilibrium there was before, it was collapsing. As the crowd closed in, Joey poised himself like a rodent in a room full of cats. His eyes flitting all over, desperate for a way out.

"—You goin to be sorry, boy."

"—You feel you could get way wit that?"

"—Not even God could save you now."

Everything faded for a few seconds. I blanked out for what must've been a second—and suddenly I was lying on the sidewalk alone. I couldn't tell what was happening. Or when the brawl began. I couldn't tell who was who. It was so dark. It was just shapes. It was just a big tussle of limbs and fists rolling into the street. Joey right in the middle of the storm. His shirt went right off, and his bare chest was hoist up like a prized hunt. The women scream and flee to the sidewalk.

All I coulda think at the time was that none of this was going to bring Sam back. Nobody knew nothing. They was just looking for something to destroy. Whoever wasn't participating wasn't speaking up. Nobody was gonna ring the police.

Three men sprinted up the street, a hammer and spanner in hand. Right in the street, they yanked Joey's pants off and bound his wrists with what looked like an old fishing line.

Joey puffed his chest up, looking like he was about to get baptized.

One of the men cupped Joey's chin between their fingers and started punching his temples. Left, right, left, right, left, right. Joey's head going like a metronome, his eyes closed like he was in meditation. Like he disconnected himself from his own flesh. The men wasn't stopping. They couldn't break him. It got so bad that the men start to fight among themselves. This one not doing it right, that one doing it too soft. Squabbling for the opportunity to lay down the next punch.

A woman came bustling up with a big jar of pepper sauce and everybody started to laugh. Boss Das was the one who pried open

Joey's mouth and the woman tilted the jar, pouring the globs of pepper down his throat. Joey began to vomit out his guts. Vomiting out the will to live. His swollen tongue lolling out of his mouth. And the crowd went wild.

I was fading in and out by then. I can't tell you what else happen. I didn't want to hear about it. I didn't care—still don't. I don't like to talk about none of it. It ain't matter. None of it was going to change anything. When they had their fill, they called the police.

And that was that.

HOLD OF THE BEAST

CHAPTER 27

JOEY'S ONE PERSON. WE WANT EVERYBODY

The next thing I remember was waking up in a hospital room, my eyes heavy and hot, an oxygen mask strapped over my nose. Couldn't tell if it was day or night. The walls was a sterile white, scarred with brown. I could see a metal trolley topped with bottles and gauze and latex. I was drifting in and out of it. I remember waking up one night in total delirium, feeling like I was seeing the walls leaking black and hands coming out of the ceiling. I yelled out for Sam before remembering why I was here in the first place.

I didn't realize how alone I was till then.

Some men in suits was at my bedside, busily interrogating me about that day I saw the body. I can't even tell you if they was police. They needed me to say I saw the body—and that I saw Joey. I can't even remember what I said. I didn't even have no lawyer. All in all, I became a witness to the whole mess. A part of me thought all of it, the suits, the questions, the forms, that all of it was just a dream. But it wasn't till later, after I was out of the hospital, I accept that all of it really happen.

There was a small TV in the corner in the room. Two elderly nurses was changing the sheets on the bed next to mine. They didn't notice I was awake. I had been for a while, feeling like I couldn't do nothing but count the polystyrene squares on the ceiling. The nurses stopped what they was doing, their eyes turning to the TV. A news report had come on.

Richard Ramsingh. Wanted for armed burglary. Body dumped in a gully. They put up a picture of his ID. The dead man had a name now. "Good! Another one dead!" one of the nurses said, pointing at the TV.

The other one was nodding. "Nice, let dem kill demself out, man."

"Exactly. Amen."

The report was still playing when the nurses leave the room.

Just then, I had a long coughing fit and couldn't hear nothing. They flashed a series of pictures. It was a blur by then but I remember what I see—

A picture of Joey.

A picture of Baram.

A picture of Sam.

It took about a few more days before they coulda discharge me. Nobody from Kukuyo wanted to take me in. Not even Boss Das. I suppose it was the wife's call. That familiar feeling washed over me again—like I was a stain. Like I was cursed and broken and that if I wasn't me, if I wasn't Rune Mathura, someone would have wanted to take me. But I had to be strong. I couldn't worry about what was in other people's heads. The house was in ashes. Sam was gone. It seem like Sam was just a passing dream to everybody, just like Dumpling was. A TV episode. I couldn't even cry for him.

I couldn't take two steps outta bed without wanting to hack my life outta my lungs. There was soot lining my airways. My mucus was grey. They say it was like someone pour a cup of tar down my throat. It was like razorblades every time I cough. I feel like I was on autopilot. But the pain reminded me that this was all real—that all of it really happen. I wasn't in control of nothing, not even my own body, my own breath. Each fit I had, I swear I wasn't going to breathe again. I felt like a balloon violently deflating. But then—the air would enter my lungs and the world would be okay for a second. For a second, I'd feel alive and feel like I could do anything. Only for a second.

They found my BMX, wherever it was. It wasn't pristine or nothing but it was still able to ride. The Joker card that was clipped to the spoke was gone. A passing dream.

They put Constable Irina Navarro in charge of me. I'm not sure how that conversation went down. She and her boyfriend was to take me in after the hospital let me out. It wasn't permanent—I was fed up of being reminded of that. My only thought was that well, nothing is, really. Being under the wing of the police had a good side. They made a deal with the officers for me to get an inhaler—you know, like the ones the asthma people have. Other people have to pay. I dunno what kinda drug they had in that thing but I swear it woulda be able to silence a train.

Navarro and her partner lived in an apartment up in the city. San Fernando wasn't really a city but it was a city to me. The apartment was small and there was mirrors everywhere—probably to make the place look bigger. It wasn't that different from what home was. Everything was just compact. It had this limp, lifeless look to it even though everything was put together and spick-and-span. Only a few days in, I realized why it felt so lifeless—it was because there wasn't no photos or pictures. No vases and flowers. Sam had paintings of Hanuman and Lakshmi in almost every room. On each table was a fern or orchid. These was things I had take for granted.

They put me in the guest room. It looked like they never use it before. The room had this damp smell of bleach that was unbearable the first night.

Navarro's partner, Cyrus, was a handsome man. Slim, well-shaven, never a hair out of place. Big-mouth people would probably pass him off as a fag—but he was a modern man, is how I see it. He and Navarro seem so well put-together. He cooked dinner the first night. I near broke down watching him do it, but I managed to pull through. He did tilapia fillets in olive oil and sweet pepper. He used a ring mould to make the rice into a little dome. He put cilantro on everything. *Pescado con arroz*, he called it.

Cyrus was always making things sound fancier than they was, Navarro said. I wasn't sure what I was supposed to call Navarro. I called her Ms. Irina once and she didn't seem to like that. I don't even think she liked Ms. Navarro.

They wasn't married and they didn't have children. It was just the two of them. I didn't know nobody who was in their mid-thirties and didn't have children. It was weird to sit and eat with them. They didn't even have the TV on. I couldn't eat—couldn't do nothing. I dunno how to describe it except that everything always seemed too close and too loud. My body jerked each time the fork rattle against the plate. Rooms was always too bright.

Navarro's eyes were on Cyrus but I know she was watching me. She was talking about the food but I know she wasn't really. It made me uncomfortable. I had no appetite, but I still tried to eat.

After we was done, they both had a glass of sangria and Cyrus gave me some local chocolate for dessert. *Real* Trinitario chocolate, he said. It had this chalky taste. But I think it was just my mood that made it taste like that. The whole situation was too strange to me. I wasn't accustom and I wasn't sure if I had to get accustom.

As Cyrus cleared my plate, he pulled me over to help him wash the wares, but he had me there just so he could talk to me. "You talked to your brother yet?" he asked me.

I shook my head. The Kangals put him up in the car yard, in a ratty shed with nothing but a greasy blanket. All else I know is that the day after that, some boys found Nick lying face-down in the middle of the road. I suppose they thought Joey put a hit out on him or something but turned out he'd just fainted. He had a concussion—he was in and out of the hospital in no time.

I didn't want to talk to Nick—or anybody from Kukuyo. My mind cut back to that last talk I had with Dumpling and how she wanted to run away and start over. And my response to her: running don't solve anything. I was probably just trying to sound tough there, if I was trying to sound like anything at all. Part of me just wanted to move on from everything. That's normal, I think. At least that's what I was telling myself. I had this desire to start over—that I could just wake up in another country and know nobody. That somebody could just move me into a dingy old room in some backwater town and I could give myself another name, another life. Navarro had this calendar in the bathroom and there was a picture of this lush green landscape with some cabins in the distance. Somewhere in Europe, it looked like. Holland, Switzerland, wherever. I wish God coulda just scoop me up and drop me off there, right in the middle of that field—and I'd just run till I find a cool spot to put my head.

"Still coughing?" Cyrus cut in.

"A little bit," I replied.

"You're through the worst of it, you think?"

"I think so."

Cyrus said, "If you feel like anything's wrong, you have to say, okay?"

"You're good to go back to school?" Navarro asked.

"Yeah, probably."

Cyrus asked, "You have a lot of friends at school?"

"No. Nobody really talks to me." It just came out—even I was bowled over by my own honesty.

"What about the boyfriend? He came to the hospital to see you. I don't even think you knew he was there."

"Who? Tiki?"

"You seem surprised."

"We're not together."

"Well, he rode up all the way to the hospital to see you," Cyrus said. "That's a true friend."

I nodded.

He continued, "You know, I didn't have a girlfriend until I was eighteen. You can believe that, handsome man like me?" I heard Navarro scoff from the other room. "My mother was a pain in the ass, a real battleaxe. She used to pick up the phone same time as me, listen to all my conversations. Other boys, they were saving up to buy a car, a good house. Me? I was saving up for the payphone."

He managed to pull a small smile outta me. When he noticed, he looked very pleased with himself. Navarro came up to us, saying, "When I met him, he had his own phone by then, thank God."

Cyrus laughed. "Irina's one of the lucky ones. But she's convinced my mother is a Russian spy—that she wiretapped the place."

"I've been through worse than your mother, don't worry." Navarro helped him finish the dishes.

Aside from dinnertime, they mostly left me alone. Cyrus had a Nintendo with *Excitebike* and *Super Mario Bros 3*. It calmed me, playing the games. Sometimes he'd sit down and watch me play. He wouldn't say anything. He'd just be there with a glass of warm milk in his hand. He didn't say nothing but I could tell he was excited to have me there. I had a feeling like this was something he wanted for a long time—like he wanted someone to share these things with. Navarro didn't look like she was into videogames. Maybe that's why he was so friendly with me.

Navarro, on the other hand—I couldn't read the woman. At times, I feel like she couldn't wait to get rid of me. But I could tell there was something behind the way she acted. I think she didn't want to get accustom to me—same way I didn't want to get accustom to the apartment, to anything. Sometimes I used to feel this overpowering guilt whenever I had a good night's sleep in the guest bed. Like I was getting over everything. Getting over Sam. I couldn't dare. I couldn't let myself.

The next morning, I woke up early. Navarro and Cyrus was always up before dawn. I overheard them talking in the kitchen. "The pig farmer gave a full confession yesterday," Navarro said. "We're trying to get Joey on everything we can—"

"Don't fly too close to the sun," Cyrus said. "You have him on the Ramsingh murder. That should be enough to put him away for the least."

"Joey's one person. We want everybody."

"He'll make a deal."

"You don't know these people." Navarro let out a sigh. "Pigs, Cyrus. Pigs. They cut up people, pulled out their teeth and fed them to pigs."

He looked down at the floor as if he did something wrong.

"Now you understand why I can't bring anyone into this world?" Navarro said, leaning towards him. He was silent. Navarro continued, "You should've seen when they brought Joey in the station. They beat the living hell outta him, you could swear he was a Judas on Good Friday. And the beast was just there, grinning and laughing at us. I swear, if we had people like Joey on our side, we would be winning this thing."

I came out of the room at the same time. It was incredible how fast they snapped back to normal. It was instantaneous. "You ready for school?" Navarro asked me.

"You don't have to go if you don't want to," Cyrus chipped in.

I didn't want to go—but it was too much staying in this cramped apartment. They didn't want me to use the bike. The coughing fits and all. So Cyrus had to drop me to school. As we pulled up to the front, I already knew what to expect, and I was right.

In school, nobody talked to me. Tiki wasn't there that day. I didn't know how to feel about that. I wasn't disappointed. I was too numb to be anything in particular. Nobody told me they was sorry about what went down—I was kinda glad for that. I didn't want nobody talking to me. I wanted to be a ghost and that was what I was. Even Alma let me be. In fact, Alma and I never really had any words after that. The only person who expressed their condolences was Moonesar—but even that felt like it was poured out of a can.

At lunchtime, my body just gave in. I collapsed right in the middle of the yard. I had the worst coughing fit since I was back in the hospital—felt like I was coughing my soul out. Moonesar called up Cyrus to come get me. Nobody even came to my aid while I was down. That stain feeling again. It's like you become a leper and they need to ship you off to Chacachacare or something. They treat you like you're some kinda monster—nobody ain't want nothing to do with you. They can't even look at you straight. You become venom even to the snakes.

I ain't never feel so lonely as I did on that day. On the way home I told Cyrus to swing by the car yard. "You gonna see your brother?" he asked.

"Yeah." He seemed happy about that.

I didn't want Cyrus to come. He stayed by the car, leaning against the trunk, looking out into the open field in front of him. A group of egrets was pecking at the puddles in the distance. I felt like a stray dog, how the mechanics' eyes fall upon me as I made my way through the garage. Car parts, tools and hoses like intestines strewn across the ground. Nobody said anything to me. Raja was there— in a navy blue cap and oil-splattered overalls. I half-expected him to make some stupid remark but he just pointed his chin to a door next to the office. The wood of the door was chipped and marked with names and cusswords as if it belonged in a toilet stall.

My heart was racing as I approached it, as if a jumbie was going to bust out at any second. I knocked, but there was no response. There wasn't no doorknob—you could peep right in. So I did and Nick was right in there, hugging his knees, his body curled up like a fetus. He was on the hot concrete, even though a kid-sized mattress lay right by him. Flat like a steamroller run over it. I felt my body back away. Like a magnetic repulsion. I could barge my way into a burning house but I was too much of a coward here.

My mind flip back to when me and Nick was young and dumb, in them backwoods where they find Dumpling. We used to be there with some of the other village children, playing red light, green light, and hide and seek. It used to be a horde of us. Then less and less children start coming out because there was talk of duenne in the woods. If the duennes call your name, don't follow the voice or you would be lost forever. You begin to fear something so much, it become real to your senses. Listen hard enough and you coulda actually hear your name through the hollows. When I used to hide, I try to keep Nick within my sight. I remember feeling safe around him—that he'd come to save me if the duennes ever come out of the river to get me.

I really believe back then that he'd save me.

So, I just sucked it up and went in. Nick shielded his eyes with his arm, looking up at me. "Rune," he said, smiling. I couldn't tell if it was fake or not. He looked liked a different person. "How San Fernando treatin you?"

I shrugged. "It is what it is."

"It is what it is here too." He sat up, scratching his head. "Whoever thought it would end like this, eh?"

"Nothing ain't end, Nick."

"I stop drinking, so you know. I had enough of it."

I nodded, reaching down to ruffle his hair. "That's good to hear."

He smiled, but the smile vanished as soon as it appeared. "You look like you holdin up good," he tell me.

I let out a scoff. "I guess that makes me a good actor."

His eyes met mine. "How you manage to get over Ma's death?"

"I never got over that, Nick. That ain't something to get over."

"You just handle it better."

"Everybody handling it in different ways. We all built different."

"I went to a church the other day." He bowed his head. "I never tell anybody."

I sat next to him. "Like for mass?"

"Nah. I just talk to a pastor. Well, it was more like he talk to me. The man kept goin on and on about this thing, the Balm of Gilead—a universal cure for sadness and misery. Something like that. And that I was using the bottle as my Balm of Gilead when I shoulda be seeking the love of God."

"You turn Christian now?"

He laughed. "No. But I say to myself that I needed to make things right with people. I was shitty to so many people. The first person who come to mind, of course, was Rita."

"Nick, you didn't—"

He nodded. "I went right up to Sundew in the early morning. I didn't care if she was gonna slap me down in the middle of the road. I waited till she arrive. When she see me, she stoop down like a dog. Then she break down, tears flowing like mad."

"Why?"

"I dunno." He paused. "Then she started apologizing, tellin me it wasn't her fault. I was confuse by then. I was suppose to be the one apologizing to her."

"What she mean, it wasn't her fault?"

He wiped his face. "She was just raving."

I scrunched my brow. He was hiding something but I let it slide. "What happen after?" I asked.

"Rune." He scooted closer to me, his eyes fixed on mine. His lip started to quiver. "This whole thing is because of me."

"Nick, what you talking about?"

He paused, shaking his head. "I dunno. Rita—this whole thing." His eyes drifted to his feet.

"Nick, what really happen?"

He hesitated. "She was just raving. I dunno. She wasn't really making sense. The girl was blubberin so much, she couldn't even talk good. Just keep saying how she was so sorry bout everything and that she was so tired." His eyes was welling up but his voice remain constant. "She tell me to come in her room. So I went. She had a bottle of Barcadi, a gift from a client."

"Nick, you didn't ..."

He shake his head. "She wanted to. I mean, after all that happen—why would she wanna do that? She start taking off her clothes and I was just there, scramblin to get it back on her. Soon she was standing in front of me, naked and crying."

"Nick?"

"I put my arms round her. I ain't know what else to do. I hold her close but had to keep pushin away, if you know what I mean. She keep tellin me that I could do whatever I want." He paused, looking at me. "I still couldn't figure it out till she fall to her knees, tellin me to just have my way and that it was the only thing she could give."

"What you figure out?"

"I think that was the girl's way of apologizing. Apologizing for what—I dunno."

"I dunno either," I tell him. "So you didn't ... Nothing else happened?"

"What else it had for me to do? She bury her head against my chest, couldn't stop crying. I never see anybody cry like that before. So I lie her down on the bed and cover her up." He cast a downward gaze but I coulda tell his eyes was welling up. "She ask me to leave then but I stay with the girl till she calm down."

"But you think it was a good idea to go see her?" I ask him.

He stay in thought for about a half minute, then shook his head. "It have so much shit behind me."

I didn't know what to say to him, so I just sat there.

"I ain't do good by Sam. I put the old man through so much shit."

A sudden weight swell in my stomach. I wanted to slap

him. Just for bringing Sam up like that. Because it reminded me that I wasn't my best for Sam neither. I put Sam through so much shit them last two weeks. But the dismal feeling wasn't so much regret for not saying sorry—I said sorry so many times. It was that I never do enough for him.

He looked at me. "Rune, you remember the day when Ma was ... you know ..."

I scrunched my brow at him. "What you mean, remember? How I ain't gonna remember?" The question was like a punch to the stomach. Me and Nick had never really talk about Ma.

"You was young." He give a shrug. "Was like everybody just shut the door. Turn up their collar and just keep on walkin. You remember?"

I bow my head, pursing my lips. "Yeah."

"Sam too. You remember?"

"I ain't think Sam walk away from it. He used to just act that way. I think he just didn't want the two of us to worry."

"That was a shitty thing he do."

"Yeah." I exhaled hard. "Wasn't the best thing."

"Maybe that's why I turn out so shitty."

I play-punch him but he move like I was gonna do it for real. It was weird, seeing Nick cower like that. I told him, "We shoulda turn to each other back then. We shoulda talk—"

"You was too young."

"That ain't matter." I looked direct at him. I felt a strange confidence. A kind of comfort that we was actually talking. I didn't even know this was something that had bother me. "It ain't happen to you alone. It happen to me too. Ma and Sam. We have to be here for each other now."

He paused, then bow his head. "I dunno. I dunno where to start."

"Anywhere. We could start anywhere. We could at least

talk about Sam ..."

"I dunno." He didn't raise his head at me after that. I reach down to touch his face but stop midway when I notice my hand trembling. I got the feeling that he was hiding something—that he knew something I didn't. "Sam ain't make the best decisions. I ain't make the best decisions. Leave it at that."

"We can't leave it at that. We have—"

"Maybe later. Was a long day."

I was upset with him. He was doing the same thing he was blaming Sam and everybody else for. Looking back on it now, I suppose I was hasty. I couldn't expect him to make giant leaps. But baby steps wasn't good enough for me then.

Out of nowhere, he get up and hug me. It wasn't really a hug. His hands just hover there for a few seconds. "We'll talk later. Promise," he say. I close in and hug him for real.

I wanted to tell him I love him. But I couldn't. The words wouldn't come out. I wasn't accustom to it, saying it or hearing it. I always wanted to say it to Sam or Nick, but I was afraid they woulda just laugh and ask me what I wanted from them. At that moment, I wasn't afraid Nick woulda laugh. I was afraid he woulda just pretend he didn't hear. Then I'd be left holding them words like a fool.

But there I was, holding them in my mind anyway, all the way back to the car. Halfway back, I began to break down. Things like that are the worst when you don't see them coming. Cyrus didn't even notice till he heard the door close. I turned away from him so he couldn't see my face. Still, I couldn't hide it. "What happened?" he asked.

"Let's go."

"Did you talk—"

"Let's go." And we drove off.

CHAPTER 28
GOOD LOOKING GIRL.

During the night, Navarro was called out to investigate a scene. Somebody had hang themself. Cyrus stewed chicken with ochro and dal. I was surprised he didn't call it *pollo a la carte* or something. He didn't like to be silly when Navarro was upset. We sat down for lunch but Navarro wasn't eating. It was only after Cyrus kept prodding her to eat that she began to talk.

"Arjuna was already there when I got there," she said to Cyrus. She paused and looked at me. For a moment, I thought she was gonna ask me to leave the table but she just continued the story, "He didn't even bother to cover the girl up. She was probably hanging there since midnight."

"How did you get her down?" Cyrus asked, setting his fork down.

"Well, Arjuna cut her down. The least he could've done. You know, I could stand blood. But it's the paleness that disturbs me. When the body looks all blue. I hate it."

His eyes shifted over to me but he was still talking to Navarro, "We don't have to talk about this—"

"The guy who runs the place—calls himself Pan." My ears pricked up as soon as she uttered the name. I swallowed what I had in my mouth, nearly choking. Navarro continued, "He was standing outside the door, going on and on about how he didn't move nothing. He didn't touch nothing. Arjuna had to keep escorting him out so he wouldn't get a heart attack. The last thing we needed was another body. I can't describe it. We just stood there, scratching our heads, gazing down at this body. And it's what Arjuna said that made me realize how upset I was."

Cyrus put his elbow to the table, his hand over his forehead. "What's that?"

"*Good lookin girl.* She was naked and dead and that's what he had to say. *Good lookin* doesn't have anything to do with anything.

I covered her up with the shower curtain."

"You did the—"

"Her eyes were still open, for God's sake. I bent down to close them. I'm still not accustomed to seeing the dead stare back up at me. I always have the feeling like they're just going to get up and start walking around."

"What was her name?" I cut in. "The girl who hang herself."

Navarro shifted her chair, her gaze turned to me. I thought she was going to ask me why I wanted to know, but she just came right out and say it, "Amrita Bansee."

It took me a few seconds to realize it. *Rita.* At the same time, I remembered her and Salaman slow-dancing. Smoke slithering from her lips as she spoke.

Navarro furrowed her brow at me. "You knew this girl?"

"N-Not really," I stammer out. The scene with Rita and Nick played and replayed in my mind. There was pieces missing. My mind was racing now, trying to fill in the gaps, wandering why she was apologizing. I asked, "She ain't leave anything?"

"A suicide note?" She paused, wincing. "No."

"Nobody say anything? Why she hanged herself?"

"It's not in my hands anymore," she said.

"Good. Then it's not something to worry about," Cyrus said.

"Nobody say anything while you was there?" I prodded again.

"There's nothing I could tell you." She took a deep breath. "Is there a reason for all these questions?"

Cyrus looked at me. "She said she knew the girl."

"My brother," I said.

Navarro asked, "They were friends?"

"Not really." And as I said it, I remembered how Rita nearly pounded Nick's face right into the living room floor. But that wasn't what Rita was apologizing for. *A man like me do anything for you.* I remember that line clear.

My mind cut back to that night the house burnt down. The night that shadow held me against the road. I replayed the scene in my head. The stink of gasoline. The heavy breathing. That *clink clink clink* like loose change jingling in a pocket. And that's what make it click. It was like someone turned a radio dial in my head and now the message was clear and at full blast. That night, when Rita barge into the house and attack Nick, the shadow was standing in the street, hands in pocket, jingling change. *A man like me do anything for you.*

"It wasn't Joey," I muttered under my breath.

"What's that?" Navarro put her fingers to my chin.

I looked her in the eye this time. "I know who burnt the house down. It wasn't Joey."

"Arundhati, what are you talking about? Joey was the one who burnt the house down. We already charged him. You saw him with the body. That's why he did it."

"I never say it was Joey—"

Navarro took a step back, her fingers leaving my chin. "Then who?"

"Salaman," I tell her.

CHAPTER 29
LET'S WATCH THE TAPES.

"Who is Salaman?" Navarro asked.

I explained the whole thing to her. In the end, she just threw her arms up in exasperation. Cyrus came in the room at the same time. He was listening in the whole time. He put his hands on my cheeks. "Rune, you realize everything depends on you, right?"

"But it wasn't Joey!" I stepped back from his grasp.

"It was Joey," Navarro cut in, burning a hole right into me with her eyes.

Cyrus took a deep breath. "Irina—"

I shouted, "I never say it was Joey! You all is the ones who kept saying it was Joey!"

"Arundhati!" Navarro exclaim. "Calm down. Joey was the one who burnt the house down. You saw him with the body. That's why he tried to do it." I swear, she wanted to strangle me, the way the words was coming out.

"You ain't listening. I ain't even know if Joey know it was me—"

"Rune, you realize everything depends on you, right? This whole case could fall apart—"

"But it wasn't Joey!" I step back from his grasp. "It was Salaman. He attack me earlier that night—"

"You said that was Joey," Navarro cut in.

"I thought it was. Now I —"

"No! It was Joey—you said so!"

Cyrus take a deep breath. "Irina—"

Navarro stormed off. She went in the bedroom and slammed the door so hard that I swear it was going to fall off. Cyrus jump as she did. I was still fuming. I asked him. "She ain't going to do anything? At least investigate it? Somebody getting away with murder!"

He was still looking at the door. "I'll talk to her."

I don't think talking was gonna do anything. She seem to already had her mind make up. What anger me the most was that she was full of shit—turn out to be a damn hypocrite. She was the one telling me not to be hasty and that you have to get all the evidence before you make your mind up. I lose a lot of respect for her at that moment.

Navarro had second shift. She was gone by four. I didn't come out of the room, and I think Cyrus knew not to bother me. I waited till he was in the shower before I left the apartment. This was about six. I didn't want anything to do with either of them for a while. I wanted to see Nick. I got my BMX and hit the road. It took me about three quarters of an hour to reach Kukuyo and then the car yard. It was already dark.

When I got there, I saw Tiki lying on the hood of an old busted-up Cortina, gazing up at the sky. The full moon was out that night, like a big bright coin in the hazy sky. Still, he spotted me as I came in through the gate. As he did, he jumped off and walked up to me. Without saying anything, he held me. And I held him back, burying my head against the crook of his shoulder. You know, for that quiet moment, his fingers in my hair, my palms brushing up and down his back, it felt like this whole mess would sort itself out. It felt like I would be okay.

I pulled away to look at him. And I kissed him—on the mouth. It was the first time I ever kissed a boy. It wasn't romantic. At least, I think so. It was just because I was so happy to see him. I hadn't realized how much time had passed. He was too startled to kiss me back. I didn't mind. When I pulled away again, his eyes was wide open. "Well, it's nice to see you too," he said.

I laughed. "I wasn't expecting you to be here."

Then he kissed me. I tiptoed against him. Then started coughing like crazy. I pulled away and he was just watching me, helpless. After I used the inhaler, it stopped. "You okay?" Tiki asked.

"Yeah. Don't worry—it's not you. It's me." I gave him a smile.

"My self-esteem gone down the drain there."

"Well, guess what? I ain't even come to see you," I told him, chuckling. "I'm here for my brother."

His smile quickly faded. "He been gone since morning."

My smile as well. "Gone? Where?"

He shrugged. "I dunno. He's usually all over the place. Just roaming about. I ain't blame him. What he gonna do here?"

"Sam wanted him to work here."

"Nick want to work here?"

"He say he stop drinking. The work might do him good."

He paused. "You sure he stop drinking? Some of the boys said they see him at Flambeau. Apparently he had some words with Salaman. Or Salaman had some words with him, not sure."

"Salaman? You sure?"

"He seem pretty normal this morning. Raja come in early, saw him scouring for parts."

Raja came up from the sheds. Tiki called out to him, asking him, "Salaman was here this morning, right?"

"I dunno why Salaman just don't sell that Roadster to somebody who could take care of it," Raja said, sipping the beer in his hand. "Like me."

I wondered if Raja knew about Rita but I decided not to bring it up. "You hear from Nick?" Tiki asked Raja.

"Nick is roaming the land again, like that man from *Kung Fu*," Raja said, taking a sip. "He comes when he comes, he goes when he goes. He better come back before we close up or he gonna have to sleep outside."

"He ever come back this late?" I asked.

They both hesitated, then shook their heads. That's when my gaze drifted up to the CCTV camera perched on the side of the shed. "You didn't see him this morning?"

Tiki scrunched his brow. "What you getting at, Rune?"

I looked at Raja. "We can watch the tapes?"

"The security tapes? Look, the big man ain't even here and it was a long day today."

Tiki cut in, "What kinda friend are you? It can't hurt to watch."

Raja sucked his teeth. "What you expect to see?"

"It'll put my mind at ease. I lose my grandfather. I just looking out for my brother."

"Raja, do it," Tiki said.

We all went into the office and huddled around the monitor. Raja was mumbling the whole time as if we had ask him to push a blasted boulder up a hill. He played back the footage from the morning, showing Salaman driving into the compound. He park the Roadster near the shed and opened the trunk. He got something out of it.

"What's that?" Tiki said, squinting.

Raja furrowed his brow. "I dunno. It look like a crowbar."

Tiki scrunched up his face. "What the hell he doing with a crowbar?"

The video then showed Salaman going into the shed but the angle obscured everything else for a good minute or two. When he came back into view, he was tugging on something. Tiki asked, "What the hell he doing now?"

"Oh shit," Raja murmured, biting his nails. Salaman was dragging Nick back to the Roadster. He was still moving. Salaman then lifted his body into the trunk and slammed it shut. Only a few seconds later, the video showed Raja walking by.

"You was right there?" Tiki cried out.

"What the hell!" Raja exclaimed. "I didn't see none of it, swear!" The video went on, showing Salaman walking to the heaps of scrap metal in the back. "That was when the asshole tell me he lookin for parts!"

Tiki blurted out, "We have to call the police!"

Raja kept carrying on, "Shit! I dunno how that slip right under me!"

I leaned my hand against the wall, my hand on my chest. I felt it coming. I started coughing again, razorblades in my throat. I fumbled with the inhaler, nearly dropping it.

"Raja, make the call now!" Tiki snapped. And Raja rushed to the phone.

I finally managed to steady myself enough to use the inhaler. The cough was gone but my throat had gone to hell. I coulda barely speak. Tiki rubbed and patted my back, tried to get me to sit. I wasn't gonna sit though. My eyes was still on the footage as Salaman drove off with the Roadster. He was in the direction back to Kukuyo.

I tried not to think what coulda transpired between then and now. Too much time had passed. I couldn't wait for no police. There wasn't going to be no lockdown for Nick, no curfew, no flashlights peeping into the cracks of the walls. Not even a missing person poster. A dog gone missing woulda have a better chance than Nick.

I stared at Tiki. My voice came out in a croak. "I need to find my brother."

He nodded. "Raja gone to call the police."

"I gonna go up there," I told him. He let out a long sigh before I even finished the sentence.

"Jesus Christ, Rune. Why you have to do this? Just wait for the police!"

"I need to find him," was all I said before I ran off.

You might call me hasty. You might call me stupid. But I had nothing to lose. You won't really understand how I felt then if you experienced that. That's understandable. You could get high on a feeling like that if you ain't careful. And now that I say that out loud—I think that's a good way to place my mindset that night.

CHAPTER 30

FIRST THE FIRE, NOW THE WATER.

I lay my bike against the wire fence. The Roadster was at the front, and the gate was open. In the overgrown yard was a galaxy of dragonflies. Stumbling across the street was a blind dog, inches away from walking headfirst into a light pole. I looked up at the house and I swear, the house was looking back down at me. The house itself seemed to breathe, moving up and down like a ribcage.

I was ready. Stupidly ready.

I walked right through the gate and went up to the front door, putting my hand against the cold wood. The house itself was wrapped in the fizz of a soft grey light. As I got closer, I felt a hum coming from the walls—it was like a kind of dark energy coming out of the house. I had this strange vibrating in my ears and throbbing behind my eyes.

A stench hit me right as I opened the door, like rotting meat and piss. The house was hollow, still, suspended in time. No sign of Salaman. Dust danced in the moonbeams coming through the windows. The world looked bigger from the inside. On one of the sills was a flute carved from cane. The drapes was moth-chewed, drench with mildew. Patterns on the wall like maps of the world. There was a stairway to my right and shelves upon shelves of books to my left. Some of them scattered on the floor, cockroaches using them as tents. Above me, glass cases filled with wares decorated with unalomes and tridents.

There was a room at the back. I didn't go near it but I'm sure that was the room where I saw Rita and Salaman that day. There was pictures everywhere. Lakshmis and lotuses. A giant portrait of Shiva, destroyer of worlds, was grinning down right at me.

Sound travelled easy through the walls. I know because I coulda hear the wind rattling through the gaps in the roof. The sound moved all the way down the ceiling, making the walls hum. But there was something else. Wasn't louder but it was more startling. Because it was coming and going, coming and going. I stood still, hunch over, listening out for it. But each time I tried to place the sound, it morph into something different.

A soft thumping. Water slushing. Gurgling. I dunno if I was going crazy just by being in there.

I stumbled over some books and some pages come loose. Charcoal drawings on them. All of them the same thing. Men with big cauliflower mustaches with their balls so long that they was touching the floor. I held back a cough.

At the same time, the sounds returned. They was clearer now.

Thump, slush, gurgle.
Thump, slush, gurgle.
Thump, slush, gurgle.

It was coming from upstairs.

So I went up. Each step, it was like I wasn't getting any closer to the top. I coulda see the sky through a breach in the second floor roof. It was black, smooth like opal, spotted with diamonds. The haze was gone. A sky like that—you're supposed to look up in awe and realize how big the universe is. But I felt the opposite at that moment. I was reminded of how small I was, like it was the heel of a big boot ready to come down on me.

And just like that—my muscles turned to jujube. I was sinking into each step now. Feet on flypaper.

The humming get louder, like I was in a spaceship. I dunno if the sound was real or in my head. But the sounds coming from upstairs—them had to be real.

Thump, slush, gurgle.
Thump, slush, gurgle.

I finally got to the top. There was a short passage, walls with scabs of paint, holes chisel into the concrete. The carpet looked like scrollwork long destroyed by rats and time. My eyes was throbbing again—like my eyeballs was going back and forth, in and out of the orbits. There was a pressure slowly building in the room. At the end of the passage was another room, door open, grey light spilling out on the floor. This was where the sounds was coming from.

A bump from downstairs propelled my heart into my throat. I had to stifle another cough.

Not now, I kept telling myself. *No coughing fits now. Please God.*

I clenched my fists, waddling back to the stairs. I looked down. Nothing there.

I went back to the passage, creeping closer and closer to the door.

The sounds was louder now. *Thump! Slush! Gurgle!*

I breathed, breathed, breathed, still trapping the coughs in my throat. Trying to swallow them down.

I poked my head into the room.

A beam of moonlight was spilling through a large hole in the roof, illuminating the room. I froze, unable to make sense of what I was seeing. A broken bed sat in the middle of the room, ain't look like nobody sleep in it in decades. A heap of headless dolls was piled into the corner. At the other end of the room was a big black oil drum.

Salaman was next to it, his hands clamp down on the cover. He didn't notice me. He was bareback, pressing his whole weight against it like he was trying to plug up a volcano vent with his body. The way his neck was cocked to the side reminded me of the crucifix. He had this grotesque look of demonic hunger. This room was a place where things worse than death could happen.

A loud metallic thump came from inside the drum. It throw him right off. He scampered back to the drum to hold it down.

But before he could, a head popped out. Water was swishing out of the drum's mouth, leaking down the sides. The light fell on the face. It was Nick.

He gasped for breath before Salaman could shove his head back under.

It was like a knife in the gut, seeing this happen. I then realized what this was. First the fire, now the water. This was all for Rita.

I had to move fast. I had to make a decision. There was a piece of wood near my feet. A loose bedpost, shaped like a magician's wand. I reached over, picked it up.

Then I bolted up to Salaman and swing it on his head—*kraak!*

He skittered to the side like a panicked lizard. At the same time, the drum toppled right over and the water spilled out going through the passage and down the stairs. Salaman let out a bat-like shriek, did a half-turn left, a half-turn right and circle right around me.

Then he jumped on me, throwing me down backward. As the back of my head hit the ground, I shot my hand up against his face, trying to push him off. But I wasn't strong enough. He bite down on my wrist, tearing off a morsel of flesh.

I knee him in the groin, as hard as I could.

He let out a yelp, throw himself off me and cut right past. He was slick.

The floor was near-flooded now, water still cascading down the steps. Nick was still in the drum. I rushed over to him. My wrist was bleeding. He wasn't out cold but he didn't know what was going on. He'd hit his head hard, blood leaking from his temple. I didn't realize he was naked till I tried to pull him out.

Then I felt it—it felt hot and then cold.

The coldness radiated right through my neck and skull. I landed clean on my back. I didn't know what happened till I tried to turn my body. Salaman was right above me, a bloody cutlass in hand. Moonlight gushing down from the sky. The pinpoint of each star getting more and more blurry. Blood was pouring from my shoulder.

I ain't even scream. As I said, it felt more like coldness than pain.

Salaman was just a shadow now. He raised his cutlass, the thin side of the blade splitting the moon in half from how I was seeing him.

I tried to roll to the side—but then I felt it coming again. *Please God no. Shit.* Razorblades in my throat. I began to cough till I wanted to retch. I spit out a long line of grey.

Then the cutlass came down. It fell, stabbing right into the ground, going *clank clank clank!* and Salaman got knocked to the side.

Another shadow. Tiki. He reached his hand down at me—but then he saw the bloodsplatters and froze. "Rune, you could move?"

I shook my head, still coughing. I wasn't crying but hot tears was streaming down my chin to my neck.

Tiki reached down for me. But the pain was starting to set in. It was too much. Too much to fight through. "Shit! It hurt!" I yelled out, causing Tiki to let go.

At the same time, I saw Salaman get up. His shadow dragging closer and closer. Tiki didn't see him. I saw too late. "Tiki!" I screeched out in the middle of a cough.

But Salaman already had him, lifting him up to the moon, licking his lips. Tiki was gasping like a stuttering car engine, kicking his feet, kicking against Salaman's stomach. But Salaman wasn't letting go. As for me, I couldn't move. I was getting delirious—I was starting to see things. I felt like the sky was opening up. Like storm clouds was beginning to pelt lightning down into the room.

I felt like one of the bolts strike me. It brought me back to life. I held my leg with my good hand and sweep an arc right into Salaman's ankle.

He keeled over, taking Tiki with him. Both of them fell in opposite directions, like two jaws rent apart.

No matter the pain, I had to get outta here. I knew that. I couldn't die here. I couldn't let Tiki die here. Pain is better than death. I kept telling myself that. Pain is better than death. I could come back from pain. Pain could heal. Pain is temporary. My blood was still flowing. I could move. I could snake through it, I told myself. I could do this. Pain is nothing.

"Tiki, we have to go." It come out in a wheeze, but Tiki sprung to action right away.

I locked my good arm around his and we hobbled down the stairs. Salaman was in a stampede right behind us. I was too frightened to turn around but I coulda hear the cutlass going berserk, slashing the walls, scraping the stone.

We made it back to the front door and into the yard but my legs gave out before we could reach the gate. It felt like my body was crumpling. My blood was black in the moonlight. Tiki grabbed me by my bloody shoulder and began to pull. He knew it was hurting me but he knew it just like I did—pain is temporary. Pain is nothing. Life is everything. I kept telling myself that. As I looked up at the stars—pain was nothing, life was everything.

Salaman barged through the door, cutlass in hand, snarling like the devil.

Then he just fell—fell like a hand drag him down into the dirt. And a spider of blood began to puddle around his face. A swarm of bats surged out from the roof and into the night sky.

Was only then I saw the flashes against the house, oscillating, lighting up the entire street bright and blue. There was a long period of silence. I was lying on the ground next to Tiki, my blood on his sleeves, black mucus in my throat. I swallowed it all back, tilting my chin upwards, getting an upside-down view of everything behind me.

I looked at Navarro, one step in front of her squad car, her finger still on the trigger.

CHAPTER 31

YOU BRAVER THAN THE WHOLE OF KUKUYO RIGHT NOW.

"How your arm going?" Tiki asked, helping me into the car, the Corolla with the busted front. He reclined the seats and we lay side by side. He turned the radio on. 'Achy Breaky Heart' was playing.

I moved my elbow for him. My arm was in a sling. "Coming along," I replied. "Your bruises heal?"

"A while now. But you know Ma and Pa, can't shut up about the whole thing. You know what Pa always saying bout you—"

"Darkskin coolie girl going to send you to the hospital one day?" I laughed. "Your Pa is a real asshole. I ain't even care if you tell him that. You had a lil splinter compared to what I get."

He chuckled. "A lil bit again and your neck woulda go clean off!"

"I can't believe you laughing while you saying that." I was snorting like mad though.

"What else we could do? That is how you live with things," he said. Then he added, "So tomorrow is the big day."

"Navarro have me coop up in that damn apartment whole day. They monitoring my every move. I swear, they watching me while I shit. I had to get on my knees and beg to come out today. Is a miracle they agree." I was reminded that she was waiting just outside for me.

"How long till you have to go back?"

"She give me half hour."

"Well, shit. Better than nothing, right?" He paused. "Well, after tomorrow life going back to—" He stopped himself before he finish. He knew damn well nothing could ever be normal again.

"They still going with the same story?" he asked, changing the topic.

"That it was Joey who burn the house down?" I let out a sigh. "What you going to do? The police have a story set in stone. That Joey do this and Joey do that—"

"Joey do more than this and that."

"Well, even before the Salaman thing, they know how they wanted this thing to be."

"They wanted Joey and them for a long time, eh. You braver than the whole of Kukuyo right now."

"It don't feel so. I feel scared."

"If you ain't scared, you ain't never been brave."

"Makes sense." I shrugged. "This is the right thing, right?"

He shrugged. "I can't even believe you still have doubts."

"It's a lie. I was never raised to lie."

"Neither was I. But if I have to do it to take down a monster, so be it. Nevermind Joey wasn't always like this. He did enough bad to warrant it."

"At the conclusion of it was a beast he couldn't take hold of," I muttered, echoing Sam's words. "I think we all gonna meet up with that beast if we walk down that path."

"You doing the right thing, Rune, even if it's the not the right way to go bout doing it."

"I hope so," was all I said. I thought back to Navarro's desperation to pin the whole thing on Joey. Maybe the police force was tired of losing and it was time to switch up the strategy.

"Joey do what he do. Just like Salaman. But Salaman already dead, so no need to waste powder on a dead duck."

"We will never get to know the full story of Salaman."

"The full story ain't mean jack shit when you have bodies lying around."

My mind cut back to Baram making me dinner, watching Big B on the TV. The pyjama pants. It was too much. I still had a lot to think about it—to make sense of in my mind. Some of it, I still can't put in place. It's hard. I had a simpler point of view before all of this. You get to know people's stories, even the worst of people, and it's not so easy to throw them to the wolves. I felt like all of us had some kinda common thread. That we was silenced, tossed around, laughed at, made to feel ugly and stupid and weak by other people. Made to feel shitty for feeling shitty about things. And that's where all the pain and bad things come from.

"And well, shit, judging from how much cars we wash down here—Joey must've drop a truckload of bodies."

I nodded. "I guess ... This is what I wanted, right? Back with Dumpling. Back with ..." I stopped myself from mentioning my mother. "This is a sort of justice—a chance to put evil away." You could only bend the law so much till it breaks. I coulda only hope that the people in charge know what they was doing. "I think Sam woulda want to smack me for this and tell me not to be no hero."

"I think if he actually saw you now, he woulda been proud."

I pulled my body against Tiki's and pressed my face against his chest. He ran his palm down the grooves of my spine. He eventually fell asleep. I let him sleep. I really was lucky to still be here, to have lived through all of this. I coulda see Nick in the distance, slumped like his back was broken, a spanner in his hand. One of the older mechanics was showing him the ropes. Sam would've been proud of that too.

Navarro come up to the car window, knocking on it. "Time," she said.

I gave her a nod, slipping out of Tiki's arms. He was still fast asleep, the radio playing soft. I stood for a second, listening to the birds, the trees. The wind. The world all around me.

As I say, I was terrified. But there was gonna be a point where I didn't have to be scared anymore. This whole thing was bigger than me and I had to always remember that. They let me know that this was not going to be easy. That even though I was just a tiny gear, the rest of the machine parts might fall apart without me. That the way forward was a step into a long, dark cave. And as scared as I was, I made the first step. As I got into the passenger seat of Navarro's car,

I thought back to Tiki's words. The bravest person in Kukuyo, he said. The car drove off and veered onto Old Trunk Road. Halfway down, we had to stop and let the cows cross the road. As they did, Navarro looked over at me. "They found this at the scene," she said, handing me a thick, crumpled, mud-stained card. I smoothed it out. The Joker stared at me. On its face was marked,

    "For Arundhati. Keep your balance, keep moving! – Sam."

# # #

ABOUT THE AUTHOR

K evin Jared Hosein was born and lives in Trinidad and Tobago. He has previously published two books: *The Repenters* (longlisted for the International Dublin Literary Award and the OCM Bocas Prize) and *Littletown Secrets*. His writings have been published in numerous anthologies and outlets including *Lightspeed*, *Commonwealth Writers* and *Moko Arts & Letters*. His other accolades include the 2015 Commonwealth Short Story Prize and being twice shortlisted for the Small Axe Literary Prize for Prose. *The Beast of Kukuyo* received 2nd place at the 2017 Burt Award for Caribbean Literature.

TALES FOR YOUNG ADULTS
FROM BLOUSE & SKIRT BOOKS

ALL OVER AGAIN
BY A-DZIKO SIMBA GEGELE
Who Knew Growing up Could be so Hard?

GROWING UP IS HARD. You know this. And when your mother has X-ray eyes and dances like a wobbling bag of water? When your father's idea of fun is to put all your money in a savings account and make you get up at 5 am every Sunday morning? When Kenny, Percival Thorton High's big show-off, is after Christina Parker – your Christina Parker? And when you have a shrimp of a little sister who is the bawlingest little six year old girl in the whole of Riverland? Then growing up is something you not sure you can manage at all. Who in their right mind could? Who? You?

All Over Again is an enchanting slice of boyhood. It is a charming coming of age story with a bold narrative style that pulls you into it.

Winner of the 2014 Burt Award for Caribbean Literature and longlisted for the 2015 International IMPAC Dublin Literary Award.

CHILDREN OF THE SPIDER
BY IMAM BAKSH
The Spiders are Coming!

MAYALI IS A GIRL on the run. Driven by desperation and the search for her father, Mayali leaves behind everything she has ever known on her home world of Zolpash, a land of sulphur and harsh weather, and journeys to Guyana. There she meets Joseph, a boy without the gift of speech but with much to say. Together they go on a daring, cross-country adventure to save earth from the invading Spider gods and their armies. Will their warning come too late? Will anyone even believe them? And will Mayali be able to find her father?

Children of the Spider is a fast-paced adventure. The story moves from the lush hinterlands of Guyana through to the bustling city of Georgetown where the colonial past continues to rub shoulders with the gritty, contemporary world. It is a refreshing take on Caribbean myth and mythology from an interesting new voice.

Children of the Spider won first place in the 2015 Burt Award for Caribbean Literature.

GIRLCOTT
BY FLORENZ WEBBE MAXWELL

EVEN IN PARADISE revolutions can be inconvenient things.

A week ago, Desma Johnson had only two things on her mind – in exactly eight days, she would be sixteen years old and to top it off she was inline for a top scholarship, bringing her one step closer to her dreams. Life was perfect and nothing would get in the way of her birthday plans. But it's 1959 and the secret Progressive League has just announced a boycott of all cinemas in Bermuda in order to end racial segregation.

As anxieties around the boycott build Desma becomes increasingly aware of the racial tensions casting a dire shadow over the island. Neighbours she once thought were friendly and supportive show another side. So, Desma must learn that change is never easy, and even when others expect small things from black girls, she has the right to dream big.

In this startling debut, Florenz Webbe Maxwell takes a little known fact about Caribbean history and weaves an engaging tale that speaks eloquently to the contemporary experience. Girlcott takes you beyond the image of Bermuda as a piece of paradise and charts a narrative of resistance, hope and the importance of fighting for change. Girlcott won a Burt Award for Caribbean Literature (2016) prize.

DANCING IN THE RAIN
BY LYNN JOSEPH
Finding Joy in the Small Things

TWELVE YEAR-OLD ELIZABETH is no normal girl. With an imagination that makes room for mermaids and magic in everyday life, she lives every moment to the fullest. Yet her joyful world crumbles around her when two planes bring down the Twin Towers and tear her family apart. Thousands of miles away, yet still touched by this tragedy, Elizabeth is swimming in a sea of loss. She finally finds hope when she meets her kindred spirit in 8 year-old Brandt and his 13 year-old brother, Jared.

Brandt and Jared, two boys as different as Oreo and milk and just as inseparable, arrive on the island to escape the mushroom of sorrow that bloomed above their lives in the wake of the tragedy. Elizabeth shows them a new way to look at the world and they help her to laugh again. But can Elizabeth and Brandt help their families see that when life brings showers of sadness, it's okay to dance in the rain?

Set against the dazzling beauty of the Dominican Republic, Dancing in the Rain explores the impact of the tragic fall of the Twin Towers on two Caribbean families. It is a lyrical, well-crafted tale about finding joy in the face of loss.

Dancing in the Rain won a Burt Award for Caribbean Literature (2015) prize.

DREAMS BEYOND THE SHORE
BY TAMIKA GIBSON
Finding Joy in the Small Things

SEVENTEEN-YEAR-OLD CHELSEA Marchand was pretty satisfied with her life. Until recently. Willing to play the dutiful daughter as her father's bid to become Prime Minister of their island home brings her family into intense public scrutiny, Chelsea is swept along by the strong tidal wave of politics and becomes increasingly disturbed by her father's duplicity. She finds a reprieve when she meets Kyron, a kindred spirit encased in low riding blue jeans. The two share a bond as he too struggles to get beyond his father's shadow.

But when Chelsea discovers an even darker more sinister side to her father's world, a discovery that makes her question the man he is and the woman she wants to be, she must decide how much of her own dreams she is willing to compromise to make her father's come true. But can she find the strength to stand up to her father and chart her own journey?

Tamika Gibson serves up a fascinating and stirring debut novel about growing up and accepting who you are, regardless of who your parents may be. Buoyed by the rhythms, heat and lyrical lilt of contemporary Trinidad and Tobago, Dreams Beyond the Shore is a heartwarming story declaring that decisions matter far more than destiny.

Dreams Beyond the Shore won first prize in the 2016 Burt Award for Caribbean Literature.